MW01479896

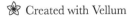

Editing: Lori White, Creative Editing Services

Cover Design: Dar Albert, Wicked Smart Designs

Proofreader: Melinda Kaye Brandt

❀ Created with Vellum

SUSPICIOUS MATE

A GRUMPY SMALL TOWN SHIFTER ROMANCE

OTTER COVE SHIFTERS

DELTA JAMES

Dedicated to My Two Best Friends:
Renee and Chris, without whom none of
what I do would be possible and to the Girls,
who bring joy to my life every single day

CHAPTER 1

ZAK

*T*oo many years living by the sea—saltwater flowed through his veins. Those who served with Zak Grayson said it was what made him ice cold. That wasn't it at all, but he suspected being a polar bear-shifter had something to do with it. There were some who said the moon was a cold-hearted bitch, but not tonight. She and the stars floated through the clouds like a ghost ship sailing the night sea out of Otter Cove, but still provided enough light that his enhanced vision could see things more clearly than a human wearing night-vision goggles.

They had to complete this mission and then it would be time to return home. Zak had been gone more than two decades, and according to both Derek and Annie, things had gone from bad to worse on the home front. His father had always been a tyrant, but while his mother had lived, she had softened his edges. But she was gone, the victim of a poacher who coveted her pelt. The poacher hadn't lived long enough to enjoy it. Afterwards, Zak's father banished him from the clan ostensibly because he had killed the poacher, but in fact Zak believed it had been to keep Zak from challenging him for leadership.

But Henry Grayson no longer had a death grip on Otter Cove. There was a proper council who more times than not overruled him. According to Derek, Zak's younger brother, their sire encouraged the young bears in the clan to try their hand at poaching females from Kodiak Island, and then made excuses when Jax Miller wanted them held to account. It didn't help that Jax had been forced to kill Zak's older brother, Hugo, when he'd almost raped one of the females in Jax's clan. Jax had challenged the younger bear to fight. Henry's son upped the stakes to make it a fight to the death and his right to take the female in question to mate. Jax had accommodated him and roared in victory when the rogue polar bear had fallen at his feet, his throat and belly sliced open by Jax's saber-like claws.

When his father had gone to claim the body of his son, tensions and tempers had run high despite the fact that it was Hugo's guilt and recklessness that was to blame. Neither had been in question, and yet the prospect of war had reared its ugly head under Henry's leadership. Cooler heads had prevailed, however, and the two clans had maintained an uneasy truce since that time.

Now, according to Annie, younger male members of their clan had been urged to poach from the bears on Kodiak. One of those bears happened to be his kid brother, Derek. He, too, had fought the alpha of the Kodiak clan and had been sent home wounded and with nothing to show for his efforts—only to be berated by Henry for his failure.

No, the time to return home was now. He might not be welcomed home to Akiak Manor, but that didn't mean Otter Cove wasn't home. There had been a time the Otter Cove's territory had included Anchorage, but Henry had given up the State's largest city to an opposing clan, not only to avoid a fight, but for a boatload of cash.

"Do you think we're going to make it out alive?" whispered one of the new recruits who'd only barely made it through SEAL training but was on his first and last mission if Zak had anything to say about it. He was a good kid, but he didn't have what it took to be a SEAL.

"Suck it up, SEAL. We have a mission to accomplish. If you aren't up to the task, hang back and you can provide cover if we need it," Zak growled through tight lips. "We get the hostage and get out. Everybody makes it back alive, got it?"

They moved the rest of the way to the hovel where the prisoner was being held like silent wraiths through the dark sky. As they closed in on the enemies' position, he spotted movement in the shadows and raised his hand in a clenched fist, signaling his men to freeze in their progress. The shadow became a man as the glow of his lit cigarette could be seen.

Zak watched as the dull light remained static. If the man was actually smoking, the end would become brighter as he inhaled and then fade back, but it wasn't doing that. Odds were the enemy knew they were out here and was trying to lure them in. Raising his hand over his head, he made a circular motion to get his men to rally to him.

"They know we're here," Zak whispered without preliminary. "The guy with the cigarette is meant to lure us in. We know the hostage is at the back on the opposite side. We're going to split up. Leo, you take half the men and engage the enemy until they commit and then bug out to our fallback position. We'll signal you when we're in place and then go on three. I'll take the rest, and we'll go in from the opposite side, grab the hostage, and make our way back to you."

His men began to move swiftly and silently. Zak motioned for his group to follow. They swung around the back and got into position, shouldering their rifles. Their killing would be up close, deadly and quiet. Leo and his men would make the noise and draw the enemies away.

Three-Two-One-Go

They moved on the men guarding the hostage, killing the one guard posted outside before he ever knew there was danger. Shots were fired from the front of the building, drawing the attention of most of the terrorists. He could hear his team's gunfire beginning to retreat, moving away from where the hostage was being held. Polar bear-shifters had enhanced hearing which meant not only could he hear it getting less loud, he could also tell the direction in which they were moving and distinguish which guns were being used.

Danger was thick in the air, enhancing his senses and making time slow to a crawl. His half of the unit slipped inside and took out two guards in the hall with their combat knives before breaching the room that held the hostage and taking out the final two. Grabbing the hostage, a downed pilot who could barely walk, Zak hoisted him up on his shoulders in a fireman's carry and they headed back to the relative safety of the stillness of the night outside the small village where they could circle back around to the rendezvous point. The lessening sounds of the firefight let Zak know the other half of his team had eluded their pursuers and had also disappeared into the darkness.

Once they were reunited as a team, they put together a stretcher, laid the hostage on it and then six men carried him to safety aboard the transport chopper that was waiting for them with its engines warming up so that once they were aboard it could lift off and get them home.

Three hours later, the hostage was on his way to surgery, and Zak reported in, sending his team back to their barracks. He knew his men; some would hit their bunks, and some would seek the soft, warm company of a woman. Zak had yet to decide which he would do. The adrenaline had kickstarted a hard-on, but even if he paid a professional, he'd have to talk, and the last thing he wanted to do was interact with another person. Bunk it was. He turned away from the 'cantina' and toward his barracks.

Perhaps she would return to his dreams—the beautiful cinnamon bear. She had begun to haunt him after the last mission. But her screams were not those of the damned, but cries of ecstasy that filled his nights and reminded him that there was another life that awaited him far beyond the battlefield.

Three weeks later, Zak was packing his duffle bag, getting ready to head out in the morning to Ramstein for the first leg of what would prove to be more than sixteen hours in the air to officially muster out at the Naval base in Coronado.

"Grayson? I thought I'd give it one more shot at convincing you to stay. I can offer you a promotion, and with a five-year reenlistment that would put you at twenty-five years. The pension difference between twenty and twenty-five is substantial."

"I appreciate that, sir," —and he did— "but in the same way I was called to join the Navy twenty years ago, I feel a call to go home. My siblings need me. Annie doesn't think she does, but she's wrong, and the trouble Derek has always seemed to find has been escalating."

"You think your father needs your help with them?"

Zak laughed sardonically. "No sir. I think they need protection from him, and although he doesn't know and would never admit it, he needs my protection from them. At some point, if I'm not there to stop it, Derek and my father are going to go at it. I have no doubts my baby brother would take the old man down, and I'm not sure either would survive the aftermath."

His commander understood. Nodding, he extended his hand. "We're going to miss you, Grayson. You are one hell of a SEAL. I never saw anyone better in the water, except maybe Pitka. That boy swims like a shark."

His CO was close, but he had no way of knowing that. Pitka was an Orca-shifter; the glacial waters that surrounded Alaska were too cold for most sharks.

Zak shook his commander's hand. "It's been an honor, sir."

"The honor, son, has been all mine. If you ever need anything or change your mind, you call me direct."

Zak nodded, not trusting his voice not to break with emotion. As his CO released his hand and stepped back, Zak saluted him a final time. Returning the salute, the man he had served for twenty years stepped back and left him to finish his packing. Zak's military flight back to the States was to leave before the sun came up. From there, he would catch a commercial flight to Anchorage, where he would hitch a ride with an old friend who was a bush pilot home to Otter Cove.

He turned and looked around the temporary quarters he'd been assigned and nodded to himself. Annie was right; it was time he went home. He'd given the Navy twenty years, a little more than half his life. He'd take his pension, his benefits, and all the money he'd saved, less the amount it had taken to buy the lighthouse and accompanying fifteen acres and go home to Otter Cove—the place he'd thought he'd left behind him forever.

The only two people in his clan with whom he'd spoken since he left were his younger sister, Annie, and his kid brother, Derek. Annie had refused to relinquish him to the darkness that had filled his soul and made him become a highly decorated SEAL. The tether between him and Derek had been more tenuous and had taken some nurturing on both their parts.

It was Annie who had kept him up on the latest goings on in the shifter community of Otter Cove.

Much like its counterpart, Mystic River, Otter Cove was a small, isolated community inhabited only by shifters—but shifters of all kinds. Their strength lay in their isolation and communal secrecy as they hid in plain sight from the human world.

Annie might be his younger sister, but she'd appointed herself his chief state-side worrier. There had been a time he thought that might be Faith, but that hope had been dashed when she had allowed his father to take her to mate and had assumed the first place among the other females. His last video chat with his sister had convinced him it was time to go home.

"Hey, big brother!" Annie's pale blonde hair was cut short in a pixie cut—yet another outward sign that she had not yet healed the rift between her and their clan. His father was old-school. Females did not cut their hair and dressed modestly. "How are you? Why do I ask? You look exhausted and just soul weary."

"That I am, but I'm fine. I may be unreachable for a couple of weeks."

"Why? Oh, yeah, right, if you tell me you'll have to kill me," she laughed. "I miss you. This is your last tour, right?"

"I think so, but on the other hand, it's not like I'll be welcomed with open arms."

"Mine will be wide open, and they won't be the only ones. Derek asked me to thank you again. Old Henry—" Annie had taken to referring to their father by his given name, much to his

consternation "—eggs him on to go poaching on Kodiak and Sheriff Miller beat the shit out of him…"

"He was trying to poach a human—not cool—very not cool. He's lucky Jax didn't kill him. He would have been within his rights."

"Yes, but then that bastard who sired us threw him under the bus. I swear the only thing that saved Derek's sorry ass was that Jax used to be a SEAL too."

No need to tell her that it was at Jax's urging he had decided to come home. Jax feared that Old Henry might be trying to resurrect a clan war between the polar bears of Otter Cove and the Kodiak bears of Mystic River.

"Please tell me that Desmond reached out to you about the sheriff's position. He wants desperately to retire, but he won't do it unless he knows there's someone who can take it on. Whoever it is will need the respect and backing of the community. You'd be perfect."

"I'm not ready to commit. My being back in Otter Cove is not going to make your life or Derek's any easier. In fact, it may make it worse."

"I can take care of myself, and Derek is learning to do the same. That beating Jax gave him made a real impression in a lot of ways. I don't know that the clan would be willing to boot Old Henry out, but someday he'll be gone one way or another, and you need to be here to step into his place."

"Not sure I want that job…"

"Tough shit. You are an alpha and a leader to your core. We need you, Zak. I need you. Please." *Fear had flashed behind* her bright eyes. Maybe he was needed more than he'd wanted to believe.

He couldn't remember Annie ever having pleaded to anyone for anything. She had been the proverbial wild child and had borne a lot of his father's wrath until the day Zak had stepped in and taken the old man down, vowing to kill him if he ever touched her again.

Zak knew he wouldn't deny her, and Derek had confirmed much of the same. "All right," said Zak nodding. "But do me a favor?"

"Anything," Annie said brightly.

"The old lighthouse out on the point?"

"You mean that derelict lighthouse they keep saying they'll take down?"

"One and the same. If it's still for sale, contact the agent…"

"You're kidding me, right?" Annie asked, obviously flab-bergasted.

"No. I've always loved where it sat. I think it might be cathartic to bring it back to life. It's been there a long, long time. I think the old girl needs another shot at life."

"Okay, but I'm not getting involved until the fun stuff starts—you know, countertops, flooring, paint colors. But be advised, I am going to start looking for a great bed for you. You'll never get a mate sleeping on a cot."

"Says the sister who's vowed never to take a mate."

"Not if it has to be one of those yahoos in our clan."

"I always thought maybe you and…"

"Are you fucking kidding me? The guy is a total putz and

*one of Old Henry's toadies. Don't even speak his name to me. I
love you. I worry about you. I miss you. Come home."*

He made his decision. "Talk to the agent. Make the best
deal you can. I'll transfer money to you to get it bought."

"Can I tell Desmond you're considering his idea about
becoming sheriff?"

"I'm not making any promises, but I'll give it some
thought."

"Let me know when you're coming home. I love you."

"I love you, too. Try to stay out of trouble until I get there."

"No promises," she teased and then blew him a kiss, before
the video connection went dead.

Annie was right. It was time he went home. Faith,
the she-bear he'd thought he would one day take to
mate, hadn't even waited for him to start his Basic
Underwater Demolition/SEAL, or BUD/S, training.
When he'd told her he was leaving, she'd given him
an ultimatum—challenge, and possibly kill, his father
for leadership, or she would look to another. Apparently, his father wasn't quite as odious if it meant she
would be the first lady of the clan. Well, more power
to them both. He had no desire to lead or to live at
Akiak Manor. No. The idea of bringing the lighthouse and stone caretaker's cottage back to life was
far more to his liking.

He greeted Bud Clark like the long-lost friend
he was.

"It's good to see you Zak," he said, handing him
an envelope with his name on it.

Zak recognized the handwriting immediately and almost tossed it away without opening it. Deciding it was better to know what was in store, he slid his finger under the flap and tore it open.

Zak,

Rumor is you're headed home. We have to talk. I have to make you understand. Please don't forsake me.

Love,

Faith

Climbing into the passenger seat of the incredible De Havilland Beaver, a smallish single-engine, high-wing, propellor airplane that was popular among Alaska's bush pilots, Zak rolled his eyes.

She hadn't lost her flair for the dramatic.

CHAPTER 2

ZAK

The sun was just starting to peek above the eastern horizon as Bud lined up the plane for a perfect landing on the water close to the lighthouse.

"You're going to need to be closer to town."

"Nah."

"If you thought you'd just slip into town, think again. You still have friends here, Zak. Friends that would like nothing better than to see you oust your father as leader to the clan. Annie, Derek, and some of the rest of us made sure you'd have a dock and a place to sleep. We got the cottage cleaned out and there's a bed, a working fireplace to ward off the cold, a generator for whatever electricity you need, and a toilet. Nothing fancy, but we figured you'd want to fix it up for yourself the way you wanted it. Be advised Annie's already checked out how much I can carry so you can order whatever stone you want for the countertops."

Zak shook his head. "I should have known my little sister wouldn't just let me come home in peace."

"Hey, don't you give Annie any trouble. She loves you and your father's been making her life hell. He tried every which way to make her general store fail—even opened one in direct competition—but Annie prevailed. Did she tell you she's got plans to open a little bistro by the side door and have indoor and outdoor seating? She's planning to give them barista places a run for their money… not that there's any real competition, but I think it'll be nice."

"I'm almost afraid to ask. Derek?"

"Sheriff Miller did a number on him, but you'd be proud of Derek. He took the beating like a man, came home, licked his wounds, and wouldn't hear anybody say a negative word about Jax. Your father wanted to take a run at Miller's clan, but Derek and a few of the other young bears stood their ground and made sure there was just a lot of angry talk that died down. Desmond's going to want to meet with you."

Zak rolled his eyes. "Can't a guy come home after twenty years and just take a little time to renovate his home?"

"Some could, but not you. Des wants someone to take over. Someone the other clans, packs, and herds respect and know will be fair. He's afraid if he just steps down, your father will get one of the clan loyal only to him and go back to having the town under his thumb. I have to be honest with you Zak; it got ugly after you left. The whole town was like a lit powder keg waiting for the damn thing to go off."

He nodded. "I get it. Annie was a bit evasive about all that went down. Derek was a lot more forthcoming, including his own part in all that happened."

"I think your baby brother is finally growing up into the man your mother would have been proud of."

The plane touched down in the cove, close to the lighthouse. The water was as smooth as Zak had ever seen it. They glided up to the dock. Zak had expected something small and a little dicey, but was surprised to see a solid, good-sized dock with an area for fishing and a boat lift.

"Who paid for this?"

Bud grinned. "Your little sister is a shrewd negotiator. She got the materials included in the deal and then people volunteered to help. You'll find a nice dug-out seating area with a huge firepit in the middle. The night we finished the dock, we all celebrated and joked that you needn't worry about the lighthouse, you could just light a fire each night and call it a day."

Zak chuckled. "How long do I have before they all show up?"

"Sunset. And they're hoping you'll have good news."

"Such as?"

"That you're going to sign on as sheriff, and

maybe help put an end to the plans of those who want to start something with Mystic River."

"Good thing I picked up a satellite phone before I left the lower forty-eight. I'll give Jax a call and see what we can't figure out."

Bud sidled the plane up to the dock and Zak grabbed his duffle and got out. Closing the door, he slung the duffle over his shoulder and headed toward the stone cottage. He looked at the dumpster parked to the side of the stone cottage. He had a sneaky suspicion that his sister had done more than build a really nice dock.

Zak could feel her presence long before he could make out her moving in the shadows. "Hello, Faith."

"Did Bud deliver my note?" she said a little too breathlessly for him to buy into.

"Yep, and we have nothing to say to each other."

"I don't think you understand," she said, taking a few steps closer to him—the same number he took backwards.

"I'm pretty sure I do. You got pissed that I wouldn't challenge my father, and you had no interest in being a Navy wife. I get it. I'm not sure I'd wish that life on any woman—shifter or human. You and my father got married, and now you're here to offer me the same deal: challenge my father and take you to mate. I'm not interested."

"You left me," Faith said with a dramatic sigh.

"No. I left, and you opted not to come with me.

I'm sure twenty years ago the age difference didn't seem like much and now the old man can't handle your libido."

"My libido? It's his libido that's the problem. He wants to screw every time I turn around and he doesn't much care who knows it. I wish the old bastard would just hurry up and die."

Zak did a double take. He'd known things weren't good between his father and Faith, but he didn't think they'd degenerated to that point.

"Why?"

"What do you mean why?" she asked, the soft, plaintive note in her voice.

"Just that? You made your choice; twenty years later it isn't what you thought it would be. Divorce him."

"And give up all that I've worked for?"

"Worked?" Zak scoffed and then shook his head. "Nope. I'm not going there. In case you've forgotten, widows of the alpha are entitled to live as they always have, but they have no power of their own. The clan, with me back, might well look at me to lead. I sure as hell don't want you. Go home, Faith. There's nothing for you here. Leave me alone and no one else will ever hear about this. Persist or try to get even with me, and I'll make sure my father and every other clan member will know what you did."

Faith stormed off, but turned just before she was out of sight. "They say the acorn doesn't fall far from the tree. You're every bit as much of a bastard as he is, and I hope you both meet your end sooner rather than later."

There was a great, cataclysmic storm of thunder and lightning as Faith changed from woman to she-bear and loped off in the general direction of Akiak Manor. He wasn't sure who he felt sorrier for—his father or his discontented mate. Hopefully, he'd have no need to know what happened between them.

Feeling more weary than he had in a very long time, he entered the cottage. He inhaled deeply and smiled. His sister had been here with a cleaning crew. He spotted the battery-charged lantern just inside the door and turned it on. Even its dim glow revealed a clean interior with an enormous bed and a fireplace that had been set with the makings of a fire and plenty of wood chopped. He'd explore his new home later. For now, he just wanted to light the fire to keep the frigid morning at bay and crawl into what looked to be an extraordinarily comfortable king-size bed with an ornate iron headboard and footboard.

Whoever had laid the fire had done it so that all he had to do was move the fire screen, strike a match and he'd have heat in no time. He did so and as he put the screen back in place, he saw the intricate design that had been created. There was a note on the mantle by the box of matches.

Welcome home! Don't fuss. People wanted to. I left you stuff to eat that didn't need refrigeration. I figure you'll want to crash for a few hours. I had your old motorcycle serviced and it's gassed up and ready to go. Why don't you come into town after you wake up and we can grab something to eat. Desmond is going to want to talk to you, so you may as well plan to see him after we're done. Stop by the store; I can cook or we can go to the café.

Be careful. I think Faith is up to something and Old Henry has got his panties in a twist about what plans his erstwhile young bride might be making.

Love you,
Annie

He ought to be upset with her, but he'd never been able to maintain any kind of true anger where his sister was concerned. He stripped out of his clothing, letting his exhaustion and the cold envelop him. Sighing, as heat from the fire began to warm his body and soul, he stretched out and closed his eyes.

It was good to be home.

Sleep overtook him from the moment he snuggled into the inordinately comfortable mattress that had been made up with flannel sheets, a goose-down comforter, and a quilt of some kind.

There she was. He should have known she would be waiting for him. She was in her she-bear form, a beautiful cinnamon bear, which was a color variant of the American black bear.

"Shift," he ordered.

He'd had this dream in many variations for the past two years. He'd fucked her in a variety of ways, but each time when he woke, all he could recall was hair and fur the color of cinnamon.

She shook her head.

"Shift," he growled as he approached her, wondering why it was in his dream he was naked and his cock fully engorged, reaching almost to his navel.

Instead of lowering herself submissively and shifting, she snarled low in her throat and then stood as if to fight him. This was not the way this dream worked, if she wasn't already a naked female offering herself to him, she did what she was supposed to do—what any she-bear was supposed to do when faced with her fated mate ordering her to surrender.

He took another step forward and her paw, with its lethal claws, took a swipe at his mid-section. She meant to make a fight of it. So be it. The confrontation with Faith had left him in a surly mood—her act of aggression exaggerating his need to force her to yield to his strength and dominance.

"Two can play at that game," he growled calling forth his

own great bear—an enormous polar bear who roared into the sky and gave chase when the smaller cinnamon bear dropped to all fours and tried to run away.

She didn't make it far from the cottage door when he caught up with her, pouncing on her back and driving her into the frozen ground. Grasping her by the back of the neck, he shook her. The cinnamon she-bear fought to regain her feet, but he was too big for her. She didn't stand a chance against his size or his will.

Snarling and snapping, she tried to get away, but he held fast and shook her again. Fear, anger, and arousal mixed in a heady perfume that made his cock grow even harder.

She roared her defiance as he shook her a third time, and her she-bear retreated amidst another chaotic swirl of thunder and lightning as she became human once more. Zak exiled his bear to the recesses of his mind so that he, too, was human—human in a very male and visceral way. Human male with a hard cock and nothing other than lust coursing through his system.

"No," she cried, trying to get him off her.

"Yes," he snarled, wrapping his arm around her waist while admiring her curvaceous figure.

He slipped his other hand beneath her to tug and pinch at her nipples, while he spread her legs as he positioned himself directly behind her. Her swollen folds and the slick that glistened around the opening to her pussy called to him as nothing ever had. He traced his finger down the midline of her body, briefly circling her clit before it too got tugged and pinched.

She moaned, but not in a painful way. It seemed his mate liked her pleasure a little on the rough side. That was good, because right now that was all he could offer her. There would come a time when he slowly explored her body in the firelight, making her call out his name over and over as he made her climax for him. But for now, all he wanted was to bury himself in her wet heat.

She was primed for him—her pussy soft and wet. He grasped her generous hips and thrust into her with enough power that he easily impaled himself as her body softened in his hands and accepted his possession.

"No," she moaned.

"Yes," he growled as he held her beneath him and stroked in and out of her, forcing her to surrender her body to his as he imposed his will on her as surely as his cock. Over and over, he drove into her, plundering her silken heat as she bowed her back and lowered the upper part of her torso, offering him her body.

"Better," he groaned as he pounded into her, not caring that she barely had time to catch her breath between orgasms.

He gave himself up to the intensity of the pleasure he was drawing from her body. Letting his head fall back he drove into her again and again as he began to pump his cum into her pussy, as he ground himself against her sex and her pussy milked his cock for everything it had to give.

When he was done, he collapsed upon her body, but she was gone. She and the dream had vanished once more.

CHAPTER 3

SIENNA

*T*ears. Tears seemed to be all that remained for her. Tears of anger. Tears of frustration. Tears of regret. As Sara MacDonald, she had cried a sea of tears, and nothing had changed.

That wasn't necessarily true. She was fairly sure things had gone from bad to worse and she really couldn't see any way out. Negative emotion raged within her like a tangled roll of rusted barbed wire too corrupted to even be used to keep the cattle contained.

Dry Creek, Colorado was a small town on the outer fringes of nowhere. The town had one stoplight, a greasy diner that called itself a café, a coffee shop and a gas station that sold some food staples at exorbitant prices for those too tired to drive an hour to get the gallon of milk they'd forgotten. Sara had been born not far from here and had thought herself destined for a nondescript life in a nondescript community of cinnamon bear-shifters. Not as flashy as the grizzly-shifters that roamed these mountains and valleys. She'd been taught that as long as she avoided them, she'd have a nice little life where nothing much happened.

All that had changed when the son of their clan's alpha had taken a shine to her and resented being told no. Her father had been given no choice: surrender his daughter or her whole family would be banished. Her father wasn't a bad man, nor was he made of the kind of stuff that would allow him to protect Sara at the expense of the rest of the family.

Standing at the end of the aisle in the little church, she looked down to see Kurt standing and waiting for her. "Please, Papa, don't make me do this. I'll run away; they can't banish you then."

Her father tightened his grip on her hand. "They can, and they will. Kurt assures me he has feelings for you. You'll live in their beautiful lodge. Someday you'll be first lady of the clan."

"But I don't love him. And he likes to whisper in my ear all the nasty things he's going to do to me once we're married."

Sara didn't have the heart to tell her father that he had done that while pawing at her before pushing her head down to suck his hard cock into her mouth to relieve the 'ache' he said she caused.

"He doesn't mean that. You just made him angry when you refused to go to his bed before you were married. You'll be fine."

She'd walked down the aisle knowing in her heart

her father was wrong. At first, her days had become an endless stream of meeting Kurt's sexual demands and cleaning up after him. Then, they had settled into a schedule where he used her less frequently, preferring other partners. He had insisted that his father turn over the pool house to them so they could have their privacy. From the looks many other clan members gave her, she didn't think their 'privacy' was all Kurt thought it was.

At his mother's insistence, Sara had gone to work as a barista in one of the clan's coffee shops. It was the only time she was free of him, and she often put in more hours than she needed just to avoid being alone with Kurt. She pulled up to the side gate into the pool area. She needed to leave, needed to face whatever humiliation he had in store for her tonight. His parents were gone for the weekend, which meant Kurt could do as he pleased without having his father interfere.

She noted the beat-up Kia Soul parked outside the gate as well. Swell, she thought, just what I need —Zoe Cooper. This wouldn't be the first time Kurt wanted a threesome, but did he have to pick Zoe, who made no secret of the fact that she wanted Sara's place in Kurt's bed. That was fine with Sara, only Kurt's father had put his foot down. There would never be a divorce.

"Hey, baby. You're awfully late getting home," drawled Kurt with his arm around Zoe.

"With your mother out of town, there was a lot to do. I had to stay and close down the barista."

"The Daily Grind is no 'barista,' it's just a coffee shop, nothing more than a glorified kiosk," sneered Zoe, who was really a horrible person and whose father had given her a local, successful café that she'd managed to run into the ground.

"Maybe not, but at least we don't give people food poisoning on a regular basis," Sara had snarked back before putting away the few groceries she'd picked up.

Taking a deep breath, she left the kitchen heading for their bedroom, where she hoped and prayed she'd be left alone. No such luck. Kurt followed her, standing in the doorway and leaning against the frame. He hooked his thumb through the belt loop of his worn jeans and smiled a smile she had come to dread. This was going to be even worse than she thought. Maybe taking a beating for not coming home until he was too drunk and had passed out might have been the better option.

"What do you want, Kurt? I'm tired and really don't want…"

What she wanted obviously never occurred, or at least had no importance, to him as his hand cracked across her face, cutting off her sentence and dazing her as he fisted her hair and dragged her back toward the living area.

"You're going to come back in here and suck my

cock while I eat Zoe's pussy. Then I'm going to fuck Zoe while you sit and watch."

Something snapped in Sara—a quantum disconnect between what was safe and what was not. It felt like a precursor to a shift, although she had no thought to call her she-bear forward. All she wanted was to end this farce and it didn't matter how. If her or Kurt's death was the result, she could calmly accept that as part of what needed to happen. She'd had enough and she was done. All her life she'd done whatever she was told, regardless of how much damage—emotional or physical—she was asked or forced to endure.

"No, I don't think I will."

"You what?" he snarled.

Everything inside her that had been roiling for so many years had gone perfectly still. "I said, I don't think I will. I'm not going to give you another blow job, and I'm sure as hell not going to give you one and then watch you fuck another she-bear. If you and Zoe want to be together, so be it. Bring her in here and bang her all night in our bed. I don't care anymore, Kurt. I really don't. I'm just done."

He drew his hand back to slap her again and all the quiet that had been within her rushed forward in a split second as her she-bear roared to life, taking over and coming to the fore in an enormous explosion of loud claps of thunder and sparking lightning. Some shifters had beautiful, magical shifts of dazzling lights and swirling mists. Not bears. Bears shifted with thundering explosions that left the unaware frightened.

Sara bounded through the house, crashing through the front window, galloping across the patio and leaping to hang her front paws over the fence before pulling herself over and dropping to the ground. She thought about getting her car, but realized if she shifted back, she had no clothes, and her wallet and keys were in the house.

She had clothes at the Daily Grind, so she charged across the barnyard and barreled through the fences, managing to impale herself on a piece of railing. It didn't matter. All that mattered was freedom. She could almost taste it. A plan was formulating in her mind. She would break into the coffee shop where she kept a change of clothes, steal some money from the till and drive the delivery van somewhere, anywhere, she could find a bus or a train that would take her away. The need to escape was... A pain in her flank radiated throughout her being. She meant to slow down, to see what had hit her, but blackness enveloped her, and she fell forward, her muzzle plowing a trough in the soft dirt.

Sara couldn't see, couldn't feel; everything had gone cold. Cold was all right. Cold could kill you. If she wasn't going to escape, she'd just as soon be dead. And it would be a better death than the one Kurt would inflict upon her. With his parents gone, there would be no one to restrain him. Other members of the clan might not approve of the way he treated her, but no one was going to stand against the bear who would one day be alpha.

The last sound she heard was a laughing Kurt saying, "That'll leave a mark." And then everything went blank.

Somewhere in the dim recesses of her mind, she could hear her she-bear calling to her—a low mournful noise that entreated her to stay. But staying meant being with Kurt, and the thought of that she could not abide. Her she-bear's long, sorrowful moan beseeched her to stay and was interrupted by several beeps and bleeps as first sound, and then sight returned to her.

"Sara? Sara? Can you hear me?" a feminine voice she didn't recognize permeated her muddled brain.

"Who… who are you?"

"A friend. My name doesn't matter. We don't have much time. You've been in a coma. Your husband said you were thrown from a horse and dragged."

"Kurt lied. What am I doing here? Where am I?"

"The county hospital, and we figured as much. We also figured if he was capable of doing this, he was capable of killing you. We don't think you were supposed to survive. We've been careful. We've been doctoring the reports so that it doesn't look like you'll survive your injuries. We've got to get you out of here. Come on."

The woman, whoever she was, vastly overestimated Sara's ability to do anything but let death claim her. The woman helped her to sit up and swing her legs over the edge of the bed. Apparently, the woman wasn't easily deterred.

"What happened?"

"As near as we…"

"Who is this we you keep talking about?"

"Those of us who help women—shifters like you. We operate in the shadows and do what we can, when we can. As near as we can figure, something went down between you and Kurt, you shifted, crashed through the window and tried to run. That bastard darted you and then beat the shit out of you. There was a lot of internal bleeding, a few cracked ribs, a broken nose and a hard bump to your head. The nurse who alerted us thinks he tried to cave your skull in with a rock."

"No wonder I feel like shit," Sara said, trying to inject a moment of levity.

"Well, that and the major surgery. The ribs and nose are healing, and the surgery took care of the bleeding, but as I said, we've been dummying up the reports. Your mate thinks he's just waiting for you to die. We need to get you out of here. Do you think you can try?"

For the first time since her father had dragged her down the aisle and delivered her into hell and the devil's arms, Sara felt something solidify in her the same way she had felt it snap. "If you've got a way for me to escape, I've got the will to do it. Get these IV's out of me; if we can get to the staircase…"

Another woman she hadn't noticed before now laughed. "You said she was feisty. Well, feisty isn't going to get you down those stairs or out of this hospital. A body bag and gurney will get you to the elevator and down to the morgue, though, where there's a transport van from the funeral home that will get you to the train."

"I have no clothes…" started Sara.

"That's all been arranged. We have some clothing, cash, and a new identity—enough to get you far away from here and begin a new life. None of us have all the pieces to your new identity and you'll have to pay cash for your ticket, but at this time of day there are lots of crowds and trains leaving every few minutes. Go somewhere you've never had any interest in going, never even mentioned to anyone. You can tell no one where you've gone or who you've become. Go and make a new life for yourself."

"Why?"

She smiled. "Because you have no choice. He'll kill you if he gets a chance, and if he realizes you're alive and he can find someone who knows where you've gone and who you've become, he'll kill them, too."

"What about you?"

"We work in the shadows. No one knows who we

are or how we operate, but if you're going to go, it has to be now."

They helped her up onto the gurney and inside the body bag. She could feel them settling a sheet over her so that her 'corpse' wouldn't upset people as she went by. There was something oddly comforting about having the bag zipped closed and the sheet covering her. It was as if they had put a shroud over her old life and she was about to start anew.

For the first time in as long as she could remember, Sara felt as though she had a shot at freedom, at happiness. She meant to make the most of this second chance she was being given.

CHAPTER 4

ZAK

*Z*ak tried in vain to stop those who wanted to welcome him home from doing so. It seemed his little sister was something of a tsunami and trying to undo her well-laid plans was a bit like standing at the edge of a dock and shouting at a hurricane.

The caterers—he didn't even want to know where they came from or how much this was going to cost him as he was sure Annie was charging it all to him— showed up about three and began setting up. Although he would never admit it to her, as it might tarnish his grumpy reputation, he was actually starting to warm to the idea of a party and seeing people he hadn't seen in over two decades.

Annie came bounding into the house shortly after the caterers arrived. "Aren't they great? Asher Wells' mate is providing it. I mean she didn't donate it, but I do think we're getting a pretty deep discount. Have you tried the goat cheese and sundried tomato brioche? It's heavenly. And for those of you who insist on meat, she also has some with rare prime rib and horseradish. All of the sweets are done by the new guy who took over Scott Hardaway's bakery. Apparently, he and his mate Kyra—you know Colby's little sister—are on the run. It's all very hush-hush."

Zak laughed. "If it's all so hush hush, how the hell do you know about it?"

"Because in my role of sole proprietor of Grayson's Good Grocery and Mercantile…"

"How did you come up with that name?"

"I googled ideas for mercantile store names and then added Grayson's on the front of it."

Zak shook his head, wrapping his little sister in his arms. "I missed you, Annie. I don't think I knew how much until right this minute."

She hugged him back with every bit of strength she possessed. "I missed you, too. So did Derek. He said he'd be here, but he might be running late. I did tell our sire we would be gathering here."

"Does that mean you invited him?

"I don't know that I'd say it was that direct, but if he wants to come, he can. I invited Jax, as well."

Zak rolled his eyes and groaned. "You little troublemaker. You're just hoping to see Jax and Henry go at it again."

"Look at it this way; if they do get into it, you'll

have a chance to show everyone what a great sheriff you would be."

"Who says I want to be a great sheriff?"

"Pretty much everyone who knows you. What the hell else are you going to do?"

"I retired with a pretty good pension. Bud said he's got people always looking for a wilderness guide. He thought I could do very well."

"Of course, you could," she said. "I've never known you to try your hand at anything you weren't good at."

"What about you? What are you going to do with your life?"

"Just what I've been doing: growing my business and figuring out how to bedevil you and piss off Old Henry. I'm especially good at the last one."

"I remember. You don't worry about him trying to drag you back to Akiak?"

She turned quiet, thoughtful. It was a side he'd never thought to see from the bubbling sprite that was his little sister. "Not now that you're home. I won't lie to you, there were times I slept sitting up in bed with my rifle beside me or asked Derek to come and stay. I know Derek's fucked up, but he's changed, Zak. I think he needs to get out of this town and find his place, but I don't worry about him the way I used to."

The hairs on the back of Zak's neck stood up as he heard a boat approaching.

"Hail to the house," shouted Sheriff Jackson Miller over the sound of the boat's motor.

"Jax," Zak said with real warmth. Those first few months in Coronado would have been a whole lot harder if it hadn't been for the Kodiak-shifter. Jax threw him the rope with which to tie up the boat and then stepped on the dock and hugged him.

"It's good to see you, Zak. I thought they might have talked you into another tour or even worse, made a lifer out of you."

"Nah, it was time to come home. I understand you took a human to mate."

"Human no more, but yes, I found my fated mate. I'm afraid I'm in that dopey stage where I want everyone to be as happy. How about you?"

Zak chuckled. "Funny you should mention that. There's a cinnamon bear that keeps appearing in my dreams."

"Cinnamon bear, huh? It's rare to see one of them this far north, but they're said to be beautiful."

Zak nodded. "She has hair the color of cinnamon, flashing eyes, killer curves. I can sense that she's everything I want, and yet I know nothing about her."

"Don't worry. If she's the one and you're having dreams about her, she's bound to show up."

"I hate to admit this, but it's one of the reasons I decided to come home. I didn't want her to be waiting for me, wondering if I'd make it back."

Jax smiled. "I'll tell you; your priorities change

when your fated mate comes sashaying into your life. And they change for the better."

"Did you really just say 'sashaying?' Brother, you are losing it."

"As fast as I possibly can," Jax laughed. "Desmond wanted me to get here early to see if I can't persuade you to become sheriff of Otter Cove. It makes a lot of sense and frankly it would make my job easier. I think between the two of us, we could deescalate some of the remaining tensions and I wouldn't have to deal with your father. Man, he can be an old bastard when he tries."

"Don't kid yourself. He can be an old bastard even when he doesn't try. Annie mentioned Kyra is no longer with you."

"No. She and her fated mate felt the need to leave town. If it was anyone but Scott, I'd have done something to stop them, but I'm not sure I could have."

Both men stopped talking as they sensed another's approach. It was Desmond Wellington, the leader of the wolverine-shifters and Otter Cove's sheriff. "I hope he's talked you into taking over, Zak. We need a man with your leadership skills, not to mention the ability to knock heads together when the young lads get out of line."

"He's got your back on this one, Des."

"Good, the young male bears in your clan aren't going to listen to me much longer. I'm getting on in years and a wolverine has never been a good match for a determined polar bear. Jax here has done his best since your older brother challenged him to a duel to the death for that Kodiak he almost raped. That was bad business."

"I blame my father for that. He incited him to do it and then egged him on. The fact that Old Henry, as my sister likes to refer to him, wouldn't have considered it rape but more of a forceable claiming, is even worse. I disagree with that idea, but I'm not sure my brother did." He turned to Jax. "Has she recovered?"

Jax nodded. "Yes, and she is actually starting to turn her thoughts to being courted. I made it known among my clan that anybody wanting to even think about taking her to mate needed to understand that they'd have to negotiate with me."

"That should have made all but the most stouthearted of them think twice."

"It did. But your being home and our being known as friends can only help ease the tension. If you're in charge as sheriff, that will be a benefit, as well. I have to tell you, my clan isn't going to tolerate another incident as serious as that one. One of the reasons the whole thing didn't blow up after Derek came raiding was that not many people knew about it."

"Yeah, I need to thank you for that. You'd have been within your rights to challenge him…"

"Especially as it was my fated mate he was after— mind you, he didn't know that's who she was, and honestly, he needs to be careful around Autumn. She can be mean when she has a mind to and thinks nothing of handing a guy's balls to him."

Zak laughed. "Leave it to you to take on a savage mate."

"And I hear she thinks nothing of tranquilizing people when they piss her off."

"I keep threatening to take the darts away from her. Doc points out that knowing Autumn, she'd just switch to bullets."

"What a hellion," said Zak, more than a little envious of Jax having such a spirited mate.

"That she is, and all kinds of fun. I wish you good hunting. Now why don't you be a good little polar bear and agree to be sheriff so I can snatch some goodies and get home to my little firebrand."

"Yeah, Zak, take pity on an old man and a horny one and say yes."

Zak started laughing. "Why did I even think I had a choice? You two and then Annie going on and on."

"Good. I'm glad that's settled," said Des as he looked to Jax, over to Zak, and back again. "I take it you haven't floated your other little proposal by him."

Raising his eyebrows, Zak said, "What other little proposal?"

"I thought I'd at least let you get the badge on him." He turned to Zak. "I have an idea that's a bit out there. Your brother was good in our fight—strong, tenacious, and he knew when to back down. The kid thinks. I've lost Kyra as my deputy, and I thought maybe you and I could talk him into coming to work for me."

Zak started to laugh, but when he saw Jax was serious, he paused. "He comes poaching in your territory, goes after your fated mate, gets in a fairly serious fight with you, and you want to offer him a job?"

"Pretty much. Actually, it was Autumn's idea. She hates that there's so much bad blood between our clans and thinks we're all safer if we're more unified."

"Smart and spirited. You, my brother, scored way out of your league."

"I did, indeed," agreed Jax. "Give it some thought, Zak. I think it's an idea worth considering."

"I do, as well."

"What's an idea worth considering?" asked Derek, as he sauntered up to join them, extending his hand to Jax. "I know there was that whole formal apology, but I want you to know how much I regret my actions and am grateful you didn't tear me limb from limb."

Zak watched as Jax clasped his brother's hand and shook it. "I'm not sure that would have been all that easy. I got in some lucky blows. You accounted yourself well for an untrained bear up against a former commando. But just how grateful are you?"

"Very," said Derek. "What did you have in mind?"

"Like I said, you gave a good account of yourself. You were smart and when you knew you were beat, you backed off. Those are good qualities to have in a deputy. And I'm in need of one. I thought with your brother as sheriff…"

Derek grinned at him. "Shit, you agreed?"

"I didn't think it would be an issue for you," said Zak, a bit perplexed.

"Oh, I knew you'd agree. You're all honor, loyalty, duty, and the rest of that shit, so you not saying yes was never going to happen. I just thought you'd make 'em sweat a bit." He turned back to Jax. "If you're serious, I'm in."

"Your father will be pissed," warned Desmond.

"And yet another reason I want to do it. No, seriously, it makes sense. The younger brother of the Otter Cove sheriff becomes a deputy in Mystic River. It might give the hotheads on both sides something to think about."

"Says one of the leading hotheads," teased Zak, who was beginning to see the changes Annie had alluded to.

"One of the former leading hotheads who damn near got his head torn off by said sheriff of Mystic River. In all honesty, Jax, I'd be honored to be your deputy."

Desmond grinned. "Now this is what I call a party. I get to retire; Zak becomes sheriff; and Derek heads to Mystic River as Jax's new deputy. Yep, this is a banner day for me, and ought to set Old Henry off like a big firecracker. You might want to stick around, Jax. I think things are about to get interesting."

Jax looked at Zak. "I can stay if you need."

Zak shook his head. "I can handle Old Henry; besides I can give your new deputy here some training."

"Good. Derek, report to my office first thing Monday morning."

"I'll be there, and thanks again, Jax."

"Don't thank me yet. Des and I just make being in law enforcement look easy. It isn't."

"I'm not afraid of hard work," said Derek. "I won't let you down." His gaze swept over all three men. "I won't let any of you down."

"Gentlemen," Jax said, tipping his hat and then taking his leave.

"You can learn a lot from him. He was a highly decorated SEAL," said Zak.

"As highly as you?"

"Well, no, but then he's just a Kodiak. Try not to make him look bad."

"I heard that," called Jax as he untied his boat and stepped aboard.

"I meant for you to," called Zak.

Jax started up his boat and pulled away.

"I mean it, Zak," said Desmond. "I can retire knowing I'm leaving Otter Cove in good hands, and Derek going to work for Jax can only be a good thing."

"That's enough shop talk. Annie has planned this

party to be a big celebration. I, for one, don't want to disappoint her."

Behind him, fireworks began to explode, lighting up the sky like a poor man's imitation of the Aurora Borealis. The past lay that way. Perhaps the fireworks were ensuring the destruction of all from the past that might harm them. Ahead a bluegrass band began to play as someone lit a bonfire in his firepit. That seemed to be the story of his life—caught between two bright flames. One offered him destruction and separation from the ghosts that haunted him, and the other warmth and homecoming.

It was time to turn his back on the specters of his past and turn toward the light to embrace his future.

CHAPTER 5

SIENNA

*S*ienna Carpenter. She liked it. It had a nice ring to it and someday might be pretty as a monogram.

The trip from her hospital room to the morgue's basement exit had been odd, noisy, and bumpy. Her nerves had been on edge and every single stop, turn, or wobble had made her body clench in fear that they had been found out. When she'd felt the gurney's legs folding under her head and sliding into the van, she held her breath as the gurney slid forward and the back legs folded, as well. The back doors of the van closed, and the vehicle pulled away and headed up an incline and out of the basement parking lot.

Someone patted the top of the gurney above her head twice in rapid succession. "Okay, sweetie we're away. Stay towards the back. You'll find a duffle. In it, you'll find three sets of clothes with some extra bras, panties, and socks. There should be some hiking boots, sneakers, and one pair each of sandals and flip flops. There's also a nice warm coat, a hat, and a scarf. There should be a small purse with a wallet, credit cards, and a whole lot of cash. I'm going to drop you at the train station. Walk in, find the first train out, pay cash and then figure out your ultimate destination. Try to avoid using the credit cards for at least forty-eight hours. There's also a prepaid cell phone and programmed in is an emergency number. If he finds you, call and keep the cell phone with you at all times. When you change phones, put the number in the new one. Put anything from the hospital in the paper sack. As soon as I've dropped you, I'll go find a national park and burn it in one of their fire pits."

Sara—no, her name was Sienna now—pulled on a pair of leggings, a sweater, the socks and the hiking boots. She tucked the rest into the tapestry weekend bag, keeping the jacket with her and the soft scarf wrapped around her neck. The van rolled to a stop at the departure entrance of the train station.

"I don't know how to thank you."

"There's no need and no time. We've all been where you are now. Who knows, maybe one day you'll be able to help us or another who was like you. Have a great life, and don't let this bastard rob you of the idea that there is someone out there with whom you could be happy."

"What if there is? Do I tell him?"

"That's something each of us has to decide for herself. I would say if you love him with your whole heart and believe he is your fated mate, then secrets have no place there. But if you do not believe you will wait for each other in the afterlife, then tell him nothing."

Sienna got out of the van and closed the door. She put down her bag, but before she could thank this woman, whom she sensed was risking a great deal to help a stranger, the van was pulling away. Sienna pulled the scarf up over her face, the hat down and added sunglasses she had found in the bag. Her face obscured, she trotted into the train station, found a ticket kiosk and bought a ticket east to Maryland. Of the continental United States only Delaware and Maryland boasted a non-existent bear population. That seemed like a pretty good place to lose herself traveling over the next few days before heading west. She meant to lose herself in the wilds of Canada or Alaska. She wanted to avoid anyone in the lower forty-eight states, especially those in the Four Corners area, that might be willing to contact Kurt's clan. She would, for the foreseeable future, avoid bear clans, of whatever ilk, if at all possible.

Finally in a Starbucks in Owings Mills, Maryland, she found an ad that seemed to be the answer to her dreams. An elderly couple was moving from just outside of Baltimore to Seattle to be with their daughter. The daughter was flying back to accompany them to the Pacific Northwest but needed someone to drive the small moving truck across country, towing their crossover vehicle. All expenses would be paid, including a daily stipend for hotels, gas, meals and incidentals plus an hourly wage for the equivalent of six hours of driving time per day. The driver could keep whatever of the stipend they didn't spend, but the total drive time paid would not exceed forty-two hours.

After meeting with the family, Sienna was offered the job. Not only would she not have to pay to cross the country, but she could also pick up some additional money to be used to start her new life. After spending the night in a homeless shelter, she met the following morning with the family to pick up the truck, which was only slightly larger than a full-size pickup, the nav unit and the cell phone provided by the family.

Sienna waved as they left in their Uber, and she hopped into the truck, punched in the destination and headed west towards what she hoped was a new life. She had no plans past trying to get away and find the life she thought she had been denied. Her first stop was at a used music store to pick up several CDs as the moving truck had a CD player and she would no longer be using any of her old streaming services. Armed with an eclectic selection of CDs, she set off for the West Coast.

The navigation unit said it would take approximately forty-two hours. If she drove a minimum of ten hours each day, she could make the trip in four days. Heading west out of Maryland, she drove through Pennsylvania listening to music she had been unable to listen to while married to Kurt. Kurt liked metal and hip hop. She didn't see anything wrong with people listening to what made them happy. He had insisted that there was something wrong with her that she didn't want to listen to what he did. Well, maybe Zoe would be a better fit.

The CD player in the truck was old-school, it could handle five CDs and would either play each one in order or do a random shuffle. She set it for random shuffle and sang until her fears faded away and she found strength in the words of others and vowed she would never be anyone's victim again.

A lot of people had moved mountains to give her freedom and she would not take it for granted; nor would she forget what the Shadow Sisters had done for her. She took a second vow to one day join their league and help others. She had no doubt Kurt would look for her, if only to save face with his father that she had been able to get away.

The states and the miles drifted by. The second day she stopped at a Goodwill and found some blankets, a pillow, and a cooler to make her trip more comfortable. Each night, she slept in the cab at an overnight truck stop, making use of their shower and laundry facilities as needed. Each morning, she'd enjoy a hearty breakfast and buy any other food she needed and then head out again, stopping only for gas or to take a short break. At first, she could feel the tension in her arms, neck and back, but little by little as they passed through the states of the Northeast and Midwest, she began to relax. By the time she hit Montana, Idaho, and Washington she felt as if she'd managed to escape Kurt and what awful end he might have had in store for her.

Mid-afternoon on day four, she drove into the lovely assisted-living facility the couple was moving to. She pulled up out front and as they'd agreed, they were waiting for her. The daughter pulled her aside.

"Look, we were going to give you a bonus because you got here so fast, and I think having their own things in their little patio home is something they really needed. I hadn't realized that having either of them drive was impractical at best or dangerous at worst. So, I can either give you another twenty-five hundred cash over and above what we agreed to, or I can give you their vehicle. It's paid for, has a clean title, and is in excellent condition."

Sienna shook her head; she didn't want to take advantage of anyone. "It's worth a lot more than twenty-five hundred."

"It is, but I can also sell the idea of helping you out for your doing such a great job for us. It'll make it a little easier for them to give up driving. So, in a way, you'd be helping me out again."

"I'm not sure I buy that," said Sienna, "but I'm willing to say I do, as I'd love to have it, and it would really help me out."

They ran down to the DMV to transfer the title and after convincing the employee that she was not planning to remain in Washington, she was given a temporary plate that was good for thirty days. Dropping the daughter back at her parents, Sienna waved as she drove away, heading out of the city. Sienna was happy to see that the crossover had a CD player and navigation unit built in. In fact, it had just about every option available.

She was headed north into Canada and maybe on up into Alaska or the Yukon Territory. That would put her more than three thousand miles from Kurt, and a lot of it was wild country. She had yet to decide whether or not she would actually return to civilization. At the moment, the freedom she might find as a bear had a great deal to recommend it.

Sienna headed north up Interstate 5 and crossed into Canada via the Peace Arch Border Crossing, the main entry from Washington State into British Columbia. The border guards were helpful and courteous and never questioned her identity papers.

"Will you be staying long in Canada?" the friendly female border patrol person asked.

"Honestly, I haven't decided. I'm heading to Alaska to stay with a friend and needed a break."

The woman nodded. "Sometimes it's best to let yourself just coast at your own pace. You shouldn't have any trouble here. If you want to apply for Canadian citizenship, give me a call," she said scribbling a cell phone number on the back of her card. "Sometimes it helps to have someone to assist you with all the paperwork."

Sienna gave her a knowing look and the guard just smiled, nodded, and waved her on. When she'd told the guard she had a friend in Alaska, that wasn't necessarily a lie. She did, but Annie Grayson had no idea that Sienna was on the run. Annie had talked about her home in Otter Cove in such glowing terms, but it was a shifter community. No cinnamon bears, but plenty of polar bears and grizzlies—not the safest place for her.

They'd lost touch after Sienna—she had begun to think of herself solely in terms of her new name about halfway across the United States—had been forced into marriage with Kurt. She told herself that reaching out to Annie would be foolish, but she was lonely and regretted the distance that she had allowed to develop. She could call Annie with the cell phone she planned to ditch at the next rest stop—and say what? But there had been a time, when they were college roommates, that they'd been close. There were three possible difficulties: Annie might not want to speak to her; Annie was a polar bear-shifter and the Shadow Sisters had warned her about contacting anyone from her former life.

None of those issues was easily overcome, but Sienna was beginning to believe life on her own would not be as peaceful and carefree as she'd thought it might be, and loneliness and isolation were already beginning to set in. To go from living in a clan all your life to on your own with no one, was far more difficult than she had imagined.

Sienna no longer remembered Annie's phone number, but she knew she lived in Otter Cove and, as she recalled, had hoped to take over the town's general mercantile store. She found the store's website. It was everything Annie had hoped it would be. It also meant that Annie had broken from her origin clan. There was no way her father would have allowed that.

Standing beside a trash can at one of the rest stops, she dialed the phone, holding her breath as the call connected. "Grayson's Good Grocer and Mercantile," answered a deep baritone voice.

Sienna immediately ended the call and removed the SIM card and battery. Breaking the latter in half and crushing the SIM card under her heel, she tossed the remnants of the phone away. She twisted the wedding ring on her left hand. On impulse, she removed it and tossed it too into the trash. Once she was back in her little crossover, she fired up the new pre-paid cell phone and brought back up the store's website.

There was a note from Annie, whose picture showed her looking the same as she always had—short blonde hair and bright shining eyes. No way was she married to some growly alpha type. Male bears preferred that their women keep their hair long. Kurt had insisted that she bleach hers blonde, which had resulted in it being a strawberry-blonde color. Maybe she would find a colorist and have it returned to its natural cinnamon color. The note indicated she was considering adding a barista, serving coffee, tea and limited pastries. Annie had to be planning to either hire someone or have the food brought in. It wasn't that Annie couldn't cook; she just didn't like to.

Maybe it was worth going to see her old friend. It would be good to see a familiar face, and maybe, just maybe she'd find a place to rest and start over. She keyed in her new destination… *Otter Cove, here I come.*

CHAPTER 6

*A*nnie ran down to join them, inserting herself between Zak and Derek and linking her arms through theirs. Des grinned at them and then split off to go join his family.

"I hope it wasn't something I said or did," said Annie. "You all looked so serious down there. I never expected to see Sheriff Miller here."

"Jax and I were both in the Navy and were friends. He's a good man."

"He would have been within his rights to tear my head off," said Derek. "I'm glad he didn't but in retrospect he could have."

"Then why all the serious faces?" she asked.

"We were talking about precocious she-bears that need to find a mate to settle them down," said Zak, only half-joking.

While they hadn't talked about it, the fact remained that Annie was in a vulnerable position. Their father would need to go through him if he thought to force Annie into a pair-bonding she didn't want. He hated the fact that she'd been so afraid while he was gone that she'd sat up with a loaded gun or had asked Derek to stay with her. He might be able to do something about that.

"Jax had an interesting proposal," said Derek.

"He's not going to take Zak away, is he?" she asked, concern clear in her voice. "Or do something to Derek?"

"No, little sister. Jax and I are good. As beat up as I was, he made sure I was only in pain and didn't do any permanent damage." He looked at Zak, who nodded. "It seems that Sheriff Miller is in need of a new deputy. He's asked me to come to work for him."

"You're joking, right?" asked Annie. "Seriously? You told him no."

"Actually, I told him yes."

"Have you lost your mind? Zak, tell him he can't do that. I mean I know Hugo fucked up... oh, that was a bad slip, but Miller killed our brother."

"That's on Hugo," said Zak quietly.

"No. It isn't. That bastard killed him," argued Annie.

"Yes, after Hugo almost raped one of his clan. Thank god, he hadn't claimed her fully and turned her. Our dear older brother, who if you recall had a rather nasty temper that he often directed at you or other females in our clan, challenged Jax to a fight to the death…"

"He didn't have to accept."

"The hell he didn't. Hugo almost rapes one of the she-bears in his care, tries to force a pair bond and turn her, then challenges him to fight or die. Jax didn't have any choice in the matter, and that's what I told him."

"You knew? I mean before we told you?" cried Annie.

This was going all kinds of wrong. "Yes. Jax is an honorable man. He's a fellow SEAL, a comrade, so yes, he called me. There wasn't much I could do because I was out of the country, but I told him then, and I'm telling you now, he did nothing wrong. And now that I'm sheriff, I mean to ensure that little piece of business gets put to rest and isn't used for saber rattling and as some kind of call to arms for a holy war."

"Old Henry says…"

"Our sire baited Hugo to do it, urged him on and then when it came back to bite him in the ass, he threw Hugo under the bus. According to Jax, Henry never once called or did anything to try and stop it, and in fact, locked Derek in the cellar."

Derek's head came up like he'd scented something on the wind. "How'd you know about that?"

Zak chuckled. "Oh, you'd be surprised at what I

know, and how I know it. There are still those at
Akiak that would like to see our sire put out to pasture
and a new alpha take his place."

"Those that want that," said Annie earnestly,
"want to see you as alpha."

"Perhaps, but those who support our sire still
outnumber those that don't. But that won't always be
the case, and if push comes to shove, it won't hurt to
have the support of the Kodiak. Having Derek there
means that those in Mystic River can see that not all
of our clan are like Hugo and our father. Some of us
still retain honor."

Annie turned to Derek. "You want to do this?"

"I jumped at the chance. I agree with Zak. Mystic
River and Otter Cove need to be allies, not enemies.
Besides, Miller is good at his job, and I can learn from
him."

"But I just got Zak home."

"I won't be over in the middle of a war zone; I'll
just be across the water. You can come and see me
anytime. And when you're feeling like Old Henry is
up to something, Zak will be right here."

"About that," said Zak. "I want you to think about
moving in here."

"With you?" Annie asked. "Oh, hell to the no."

"Look, the old man is going to be pissed about
Derek and that's going to make him antsy. I want you
to know that if they grab you, you are to do nothing. I

will come for you, and I will get you out. He will not force you into a pair bonding. The cottage is pretty roomy, especially if we just go with two bedrooms with attached baths and then open concept for the rest of it. Or," he said holding up his hand, "it can be temporary and we can fix up the lighthouse, as well."

"But being upstairs over the store is so convenient."

"Agreed, but it also leaves you vulnerable in a way I'm not comfortable with."

"He's got a point, Annie. Besides, it's gorgeous out here and you guys would have each other for company."

"He won't mess with you if you're living with me. He's got to know better."

"Yeah, but I'm all about having my independence and no one tells me what to do, and now I'm living with my big brother because I'm afraid of the asshole."

"You're being prudent, but here's the thing. We can spin it that you're being your usual pushy self and you're worried that I'm going to need someone to help me get this place in order as well as oversee the work that needs to be done while I'm off being sheriff —all of which has the decided advantage of being true."

"You wouldn't mind?"

"Not at all. Honestly, if you can help me get this

place squared away it would be really helpful. I'm going to have a lot of work on my hands. I think the town will be fine with me being sheriff, but we're most likely going to get some grief about Derek going to work for Jax."

Annie stopped and forced Derek to look at her. "You really want this?" she asked him.

"I do. I've done a lot of thinking and growing up since I tried poaching in Jax's territory, and I suspect I'm going to do a bit of groveling where his mate is concerned. I understand she is quite the force to be reckoned with."

Zak chuckled. "She'd have to be to be his fated mate."

They joined the rest of those gathered to celebrate Zak's return. There was a mournful sound when Desmond announced he was retiring from his position as sheriff, which was replaced by a loud chorus of cheers when he then told the crowd that Zak had agreed to take on the position.

The crowd parted and Zak knew things were about to get tense as Henry Grayson made his presence known.

"So, the Naval hero returns. Yet, he forgets to ensure that his alpha and father is informed," said Henry Grayson, alpha to the Otter Cove polar bear clan. Zak wondered when his father had become so old.

"I'm sure you knew I was coming long before I

landed. As for the rest, I do not recognize anyone as my alpha."

There was a gasp from the crowd. Henry straightened his back and stared at his son. Nothing was said, but both recognized a gauntlet had been thrown down.

"You were always an insolent son."

Zak couldn't help but wonder what game Henry was playing. How did he see this benefiting him?

"I was always my mother's son."

"She coddled you."

"As opposed to what you did to Hugo, who chose to try and kidnap and rape a she-bear to whom he had no claim? You and your teachings got him killed. You're fortunate that Des was more indulgent of your behavior than I would have been, and Jax showed great restraint…"

"He killed my son," spat Henry.

"And kept his clan from going to war. That is not a war you would have won, old man." Zak raised his voice and scanned the crowd. "Let it be known that anyone, regardless of the species, that looks to go poaching on Kodiak will not have to worry about Jax. That person will answer to me."

Derek stepped up to his side. "And to me. Tonight, Sheriff Jackson Miller offered me the position of deputy in Mystic River. I have accepted."

A silent hush fell over the crowd.

"You have incited your younger brother to mutiny. I hold you responsible," Henry accused Zak.

"If I am responsible for Derek breaking free of your yoke, I will own that with a glad heart. But then you are responsible for Hugo's death. You incited him to poach from Kodiak—from Jax's own clan—and then after he died, you decided to revise history to make Jax the villain and Hugo the poor, misunderstood victim. What part of your addled brain decided to send an untried bear into the territory of a trained Kodiak warrior? How did you foresee any result other than Hugo refusing to back down and getting himself killed?"

"You don't know what was said between Hugo and I…"

"Don't I? I know you have done your best to poison the minds of our clan towards those on Kodiak. You've been pulled back from the brink of war so many times."

"We are the superior clan. That island was once ours…"

"How many centuries ago, old man? What does it matter? You are not some feudal lord who is owed his due. When was the last time you did anything for the clan? When did you not see Akiak as your personal fiefdom. There will come a time old man, when those in our clan who want progress will outnumber you and your faction. When that time comes, I will be here. Until then, I will be sheriff and will work with

Jax and Derek to keep both Mystic River and Otter Cove safe."

"Until then, I am still alpha, and I will see that my people keep to the old ways." The two large bear-shifters standing behind Henry stepped forward as if in response to some silent command. "Annie, you will pack your things and prepare to return home."

"You know," Annie said in a deceptively soft voice, which could be heard by all as the night had become silent except for the crackling of the fire and the lapping of the water along the shoreline. "It's funny you should mention packing. Zak asked me if I could move in with him until he gets all the renovations done and has a chance to settle in. I, for one, have missed him and his steadying influence."

"I forbid it," snarled Henry. "Seize them."

There was a massive cacophony of sound and fury as the opposing pairs of male bear-shifters changed from man to beast and charged one another —all four focused on Annie, who ducked back and away to get out of the fray. Lightning and thunder meshed with the fireworks that were still lighting the night sky over the water. Growls and snarls accompanied the gnashing of razor-sharp teeth and swipes of large, lethal claws.

The two opposing pairs faced off. Fur and blood flew as the polar bears locked in deadly combat, grappling with each other. Zak was able to see that Derek was capable of defending himself which meant he could focus on the bear intent on trying to kill him and kidnap Annie. His baby sister had been right to be afraid. He and Derek would need to teach their opponents as well as their sire that his reign of terror, especially where their sister was concerned, was over.

Zak shoved at the massive polar bear who took a swipe at his belly. Zak could feel his opponent's claws slicing through his thick fur and cutting through to skin. The wound was not deep but could have been lethal. Apparently, Henry had not cautioned them against killing his sons. No matter; Zak could tell he and Derek had the upper hand, and Henry's goons were going to get their asses kicked and then some.

He brought his paw down in a mighty blow and opened up the shoulder of his attacker. Zak charged, putting his own shoulder into the bear's midsection and shoving him backwards. The bear who had been the aggressor stumbled backward and then fell, only managing to land on his side.

"Enough," Annie's voice rang out, piercing the sounds of the fight.

Everyone looked to where Annie stood, grasping Henry's hair in her left hand, tugging his head back and exposing his throat. With her right, she held an exposed blade at his throat.

"The two of you who attacked my brothers, leave this bonfire. You and this pathetic piece of shit you call your alpha are not welcome here, nor do I ever want to see you in my store." She shook Henry. "As for you, old man, I lost one brother to your scheming. I will not lose another. If you ever try to hurt either of my brothers again, you won't have to worry about them. I will end you."

She spat the last at their sire, and Zak had no doubt in his mind that she spoke the truth. All four of the polar bears shifted back and were tossed sweatpants so they weren't standing completely naked. Shifters, in general had a more relaxed attitude about nudity, but still in a crowd of mixed genders and species, it was best to cover up as soon as possible.

"You heard her, old man, you and yours are not welcome here or at Annie's place. I dare say you were already *persona non-grata* in Mystic River. See that you and yours mind your P's and Q's here in Otter Cove. Now get out."

Annie turned loose of their sire, tossing him towards his flunkies and came to stand between her brothers. As they headed back to their vehicle, Zak shook his head and then walked into the cottage to find a pair of jeans, a sweater and some footwear. He had just entered when Annie's cell rang for her business. He knew she often took special orders after hours. How hard could it be?

He answered, "Grayson's Good Grocer and Mercantile." There was a momentary pause and then the line went dead. He looked at the screen. The caller ID said 'Unknown.' Curious.

What had happened here tonight would be all

over the county by morning. The lines could not have been more clearly drawn. He had no question as to who would be the victor, the only question that remained was how much blood would need to be spilled before it was all over.

CHAPTER 7

SIENNA

S ienna felt like an idiot; she should never have made the call. Granted, there was no way to trace the call, and she had destroyed the phone. For so many years she thought she wanted nothing more than peace and solitude and to be left alone. And yet, not even a month in, she found herself lonely and wanting to talk to someone. The idea of starting over with no baggage had some appeal and she knew she could do that—find a place, settle down, and build new friendships.

But for some reason, she kept thinking of Annie and of the town in which she'd grown up—Otter Cove. Annie's father was alpha, but Annie despised him. She did, however, adore her older brother Zak and younger brother, Derek. Zak was a Navy SEAL, as Sienna recalled, and Derek was something of a troublemaker, but Annie had always said she could count on them no matter what. Sienna wondered what it must be like to have family you could depend on. The only thing she could depend on from her family was them doing what was best for themselves with little care or concern for Sienna's needs.

Sienna knew she could take care of herself; in many ways, she'd been doing so most of her life. But the time spent with Annie had been full of laughter and mischief. Annie had confessed to her that she never planned to take a mate. She planned to strike out on her own but remain in Otter Cove. There was an old mercantile store that had been abandoned for more than one hundred years. As there was no grocery or dry goods store in Otter Cove, Annie's dream was to renovate the building and bring the store back to life.

As soon as she'd seen the listing on the web, she knew it was Annie's store, but who was the man who'd answered? Would she be safe in Otter Cove? Annie had always made it sound idyllic except for the stranglehold her father held on her clan. Sienna knew she could trust Annie, but could she trust anyone else? That question, as it formed in her mind, seemed somewhat academic, as only Annie would know she'd ever been anyone other than Sienna Carpenter. Maybe the reason she was called to Otter Cove was because it was where she had always truly belonged.

Sienna feared calling the store a second time, but she had long ago forgotten Annie's personal cell. She couldn't just drop in unannounced, could she? The pull to Otter Cove had not decreased since she'd left Colorado. The further north she went, the stronger the urge to go. It probably wouldn't hurt if she just went up to look around. If it seemed safe; maybe she could connect with her old friend. Maybe she could find a life for herself in the Alaskan wilderness. Well, it was a town and not a wilderness, but still, it was Alaska, and it might offer her just the safe haven she needed.

Heading north and to the west, Sienna listened to the CD player as it shuffled through her CD's, providing her with just the right combination of artists and songs to fuel her desire, fluff her courage, and drive her forward into the setting sun.

Almost ten days later, Sienna was on the last leg of her trip to Otter Cove. As scared as she had been the past couple of years, and as nerve-wracking as it had been to strike out on her own, slowly but surely, a small bubble of excitement had begun to build within her. She was free and she wondered if Kurt even cared enough to ask if she had died or even really look for her. He might make an attempt for show, but he didn't want her. He'd thought her barren. She wasn't. She'd had to pay cash to get an implant to keep from getting pregnant. Her father might have condemned her to hell, but she wouldn't do the same to any child of hers.

Remembering what the Shadow Sisters had told

her, she had not traveled in a straight line; she'd looped back, changed directions, and traveled a lot at night. Darkness had become her friend, and she welcomed its embrace each night. She still dreamed of a dark-haired man with close-cropped hair and the most amazing hazel eyes. At first, she thought he must be a 'book boyfriend' from one of her romance novels, but a quick review of the books on her Kindle had proved that to be false. He wasn't like anyone she'd ever seen in real life, and he literally took her breath away. Of course, someone like him wouldn't be interested in a woman like her—much less a cinnamon bear-shifter.

Sienna could have kicked herself. She had miscalculated the distance between the next two points on her route. It was pitch black outside, and there were no rest stops showing on the nav unit. She had enough fuel and wasn't hungry, but god, she had to pee. There were only two choices—find a place to pull over and relieve herself or find herself with a huge mess. Not much of a choice.

She found a turn-out spot where slower vehicles could pull over so those going the speed limit could get by safely. Not exactly ideal for a woman alone, but she opened the sunroof and scented the air for anything that smelled human or shifter. Finding nothing, she got out of the car and moved off into the copse of trees on the side of the road.

Lacing her keys through her fingers to use as a

weapon, she found a place with soft absorbent moss. Once she was done, she used the package of cleansing wipes she'd been keeping in her coat pocket, cleaned herself up and put the soiled ones back in a Zip-loc bag. Before she made the clearing, she could hear and smell the human boys who had spotted her car and were now parked behind her and were lounging around on it, waiting for her.

Poor boys. They were in for a nasty surprise. Finding a spot to remove her clothes and set down her keys, Sienna called forth her she-bear who seemed happy to be getting to come out more often. Sienna had taken to shifting at least every couple of days so her bear could stretch out her muscles and stay in shape. In the past, shifting had never been important to her. But that, like a lot of other things, had changed when she'd chosen to take her life and her future in her own hands.

In a flash of lightning and a clap of thunder, the naked woman became the cinnamon bear. She charged out of the trees, roaring in defiance and daring those silly boys to try and take her on. Granted, she wasn't as big as a grizzly or polar bear, but compared to a mere human she was a force to be reckoned with.

"Holy shit!" cried one as he fell over himself trying to put the car between her and him.

"It's a bear!" cried the other.

No shit, Sherlock!

Both boys, as well as their two companions who had remained with their SUV scrabbled over each other to get in their vehicle and drive away, their tires spinning and kicking up gravel everywhere. Sienna rushed to the edge of the road and stood on her hind legs, slashing at the night with her paws and their sharp claws. She didn't know if they could see her, but it felt good to seize the opportunity to defend herself and drive them off.

She plopped back down on all fours and made a chuffing noise, which was her she-bear's way of laughing. It seemed like she, too, had enjoyed the adrenaline rush. Sienna quickly padded back to the bush behind which she'd left her clothing, shifted back to human form, redressed and sprinted to her vehicle, where she double checked that it was still locked, and that no intruder had managed to hide within. Lesson learned. She would be more careful in the future about these last few legs of her journey.

Tomorrow she would leave Canada and once again enter U.S. territory. Alaska beckoned.

She followed the road signs and the navigation unit's instructions along the rugged coastline of Alaska's southeast coast. 'Roads' was something of a misnomer, as once you got south of Anchorage onto the peninsula, the roads were more hardened paths of gravel or packed dirt. It was easy to see why most people preferred SUVs and crossovers, although she suspected in Anchorage or Fairbanks proper a front-wheel drive car might work just as well.

Sienna thought she'd never see anything as beautiful as the front range of Colorado, but she had to admit the rugged terrain, mountains and seashore combined to make a breathtaking sight. As the roads were practically deserted, she stopped several times just to take it all in. She could see where Annie's general mercantile store was probably a smashing success. Most people probably preferred to stay close to home, and if they forgot something on a major grocery run, it would be far more convenient to head to Annie's.

She turned her head to what she might be able to do. Her only real experience was in the bistro, where she'd become a good barista as well as a solid baker. She didn't make fancy things like a pastry chef might, but she'd put her muffins, scones, and biscotti up against anybody's. She didn't have huge sums of cash, but she had enough that she might be able to open some kind of coffee shop or kiosk. Did they have kiosks in Otter Cove? Did they want one? Was there any kind of commute? Getting a loan with a bank would be tough, as she didn't really have any credit history and she wanted to stay off the grid as much as possible.

The road said Otter Cove was twenty miles. Wilderness and national parks had given way to more cultivated areas—manicured lawns and lush pastures abounded. On the outskirts of town was an enormous rock wall enclosing a huge property with an iron gate keeping the world out. Akiak. Unless she was mistaken, that's where Annie had grown up.

She slowed down and looked around the beautiful village of Otter Cove. She would never call it a town or a city; it was far too charming. It looked as though it had been here for centuries, and according to Annie, it had. There was a wide main street with a row of buildings on either side—a gas station, barbershop, sheriff's office, a diner, a small hotel—all the things someone would expect from a town that was as steeped in history as it was.

The row of shops and offices on the oceanside started with the sheriff's office on one end and a large building with a sign proclaiming Grayson's Good Grocery and Mercantile. It was just as Sienna had imagined it… just as Annie had dreamed it. Pulling into one of the parking places, she reached to the passenger side to get her purse. Sienna had the door part of the way open but couldn't get out as the strap of the purse had become wrapped around the gearshift.

"Oh, for heaven's sake," she said, tugging at it.

The bag seemed to be completely committed to its cause of remaining in the vehicle. Twisting her body, Sienna leaned back into the car, trying to free her bag from the evil clutches of the gearshift.

"Damn it," she snarled, pulling at the bag to free it.

As if the bag had just realized she wanted to take it inside, it became free of the gearshift and Sienna went backwards, the driver's side door opening wide and hitting someone. There was a loud 'oof' as Sienna fell out of the car and landed on her ass, her heels resting on the seat and her purse sitting innocently on the floorboard as if it had nothing to do with her predicament.

The car door opened further as a travel mug was placed on the roof. Sienna looked up to see the most gorgeously arresting man she'd ever seen in her life. Tall and broad-shouldered, he looked to be heavily muscled. He had short, dark hair, a close-cropped beard and mesmerizing hazel eyes.

He was also the man from her dreams.

He shimmied between the open door to her vehicle and the SUV parked next to her. Reaching down, he put his hands under her arms and lifted her up.

"I think you'll find you can stand if you put your feet down," he said with a chuckle.

"Uh, oh, yeah." *Brilliant, witty comeback.* She lowered her feet to the ground and tried to turn to face him, twisting her ankle so that the damn thing gave way and she feared she was about to hit the ground a second time.

"Easy," he said. "Are you hurt?"

Hurt wasn't the word she thought most appropriate to her current situation. Aroused and embarrassed, but mostly aroused.

"Let's see if we can't get you to safety," he said, putting one of his strong arms behind her knees and scooping her up as though she weighed nothing.

He started toward the wide front porch in front of Annie's store.

"My purse…"

He stepped up onto the porch and set her down in one of the comfortable rocking chairs. Her ankle was already feeling better, but she wasn't about to tell him that.

He grinned at her. "This is Otter Cove miss, and I'm the sheriff. Trust me, nobody in town is stupid enough to try and snatch your purse. I don't take kindly to anyone putting a damsel in distress."

CHAPTER 8

"*Z*ak? Are you accosting my customers again," said Annie as she walked out onto the porch.

"I know I must look a mess," said Sienna as she turned to the gorgeous man. "I'm Sienna Carpenter. I knew Annie when she was in school."

"Sienna," said Annie, recovering instantly after an initial double-take. "You look fine, and you haven't changed a bit. I would have recognized you anywhere."

Annie came out onto the porch, embracing Sienna before turning to the man who had identified himself as a sheriff. Zak. "Don't just stand there, get Sienna's purse for her, will you?" Annie shook her head. "I swear male bears have the worst manners. They're fine around their buddies, but let a pretty female get in their sights and they either can't form a coherent sentence or they want to go all caveman."

She wasn't about to go all caveman or cave-woman, but the ability to utter more than single syllable words when looking at him was just as scarce. As Sienna snuck a look at him, she decided he was the most beautiful thing in the world. Keep the Grand Canyon, the Aurora Borealis, the Great Pyramids, and all the rest of things people believed to be beautiful. They didn't hold a candle to him. He was arresting, arousing, and simply amazing. Sienna had to consciously tell herself to take her eyes off him. Staring would be rude, wouldn't it? Drooling even more so but licking him was entirely out of the question.

"Are those my only two choices?" said the man with the compelling eyes, smiling. "Because I know which one I'd pick. And talk about forgetting manners. I'm Zak Grayson. I'm Annie's big brother. I am also, as I told you, the sheriff of Otter Cove. What brings you to our fair town?"

Curious. Why was he asking her that? Did he know something? Was he working with Kurt? Was he, by the nature of his job, suspicious of any stranger? Or was he just being nice and making small talk?"

"Annie always talked about this place. I just got a wild hair, was between jobs, had some money saved and decided to come up to see her. It's been so long since we had a chance to see each other. I didn't have her cell phone number, so here I am."

Stop talking; way too much information sharing. Don't make him any more suspicious than he might already be.

The gorgeous man stepped off the porch, leaned into her car, retrieved her purse, and handed it to her. "Here you go. I can't have Annie convincing you I'm a total neanderthal."

"I would never think that," she said. "You're far too beautiful to be a neanderthal." Both the stunning specimen of male bear-shifter and his sister chuckled. "Did I say that out loud?"

Annie linked her arm through Sienna's. "Yes, I'm afraid you did. Now I'm going to take you inside before you give him more cause to have an over-inflated ego."

"I am the soul of humility."

"Oh, please," said Annie, rolling her eyes. "You know, you can go to hell for lying as well as stealing—just saying."

The strong, symmetrical planes of his face softened as his eyes crinkled and he laughed out loud. "And on that note, I'm going back to my office. You really need to get some help with the store. I'm glad that you've made the store such a success, but at some point, you're going to need to hire someone, especially if you want to do that fancy coffee thing."

"Don't worry, big brother, I'll make sure there's

boring coffee that will melt a spoon for you caveman types," quipped Annie.

Even the grunting noise he made towards his sister was sexy. Annie drew her inside.

"What the hell?" Annie whispered, shoving her past customers who were browsing the aisles filled with the most amazing array of items as well as some of the most mundane.

"I can't come see an old friend?" Sienna asked.

"Of course, you can. But the last time I talked to you, your father—who, by the way, isn't much better than mine—had forced you into a pair bonding you didn't want. When I called a few weeks later I was told you had been mated and were no longer speaking to old friends. I didn't buy it for a second, but at the time, I was having to deal with my own father and his dynastic delusions. Are you okay? Did the Shadow Sisters help you get away?"

Sienna could feel her eyes widen. "How do you know about the Shadow Sisters?"

"I've heard rumors about them for as long as I can remember. Then a few years ago, they helped one of the she-bears in my father's clan. I've done what I could since then to help. Nobody in Otter Cove knows that I know anything about them or will even admit they exist."

"Your father's clan? Not yours?"

"Not any longer. I walked away and opened this place. It hasn't always been easy, but now with Zak back home and taking the sheriff position, as well as Derek becoming the deputy in Mystic River, it's safer."

"Now?"

Annie nodded. "I don't think for even a second that Old Henry is going to let this go and it doesn't help that I moved out to the lighthouse with Zak for a while. I think at some point my old clan is going to fracture with the more progressive bears convincing Zak to form a new clan."

"Do you think he'll do it?"

"I'm not sure. Don't get me wrong; he'll protect those who no longer want to be with Old Henry. I'm just not sure if he'll just lead those who don't want to be at Akiak or challenge Old Henry to a fight for leadership."

"Could he win?"

"From a physical standpoint, absolutely. The problem is, my sire still has his old guard that will back him. They have a vested interest in Old Henry staying in power."

"It sounds like at least your clan will have a choice."

"Agreed. And a lot of those who want Zak to lead spend a lot of time helping us rehab the lighthouse so they can harangue him about doing so."

"You sound like you want him to fracture the clan."

"Honestly, I don't care one way or another as long

as Old Henry is ousted, and Zak takes his place as alpha. The honor and viability of our clan has been diminishing since my mother was killed. We need someone to lead us back to where we once were. The other clans—bears and non-bears alike—respected us and looked to the Otter Cove clan as an example, but not anymore. Old Henry has grown isolationist and options for opportunity and growth for our people have all but vanished. It's sad."

"Pureblood bears are solitary in nature…"

"But humans aren't. Community is our greatest strength."

"Don't you think a bear, even a she-bear, could live on her own?"

"Could she? Yes, but why should isolation be more appealing than having a supportive clan where everyone can have whatever they want as long as they're willing to work for it?" Annie stopped abruptly. "God, would you listen to me go on and on. I didn't even give you time to answer. Are you okay?"

"I am now—thanks in large part to the Shadow Sisters. Kurt, the bear my father had me bonded to, beat me to the point I had to be hospitalized. The Shadow Sisters arranged for me to get out. They gave me a new identity, cash and a start at a new life. I disappeared and headed east, then I circled back to the west coast and decided to come north. At first, I was planning to live alone. After being suffocated in my origin clan and then having my father barter me off to the alpha for his son, the idea of living alone had a lot of appeal, but then I realized I was lonely." She took Annie's hands in hers. "The time I spent with you were the best years of my life so far, so I came here. I just wanted to see you to see if I could find my own way."

There were tears in Annie's eyes. "We need to sit down and have an in-depth talk but know this. You are welcome here for as long as you like—no strings attached. You are safe here. Old Henry, if he knew, would turn you over to your clan in a heartbeat. Zak may have some neanderthal leanings, but trust me, my big brother is all about doing the right, noble, and honorable thing."

"It looks like you've got a full house. Show me how to use the register and let me help. I worked in my mother-in-law's café. I'm good with people."

"Since you don't know where things are, I'll help people find stuff, you ring and bag them up." She led Annie behind the long counter at the back of the store. After showing her how to use the register, she said, "I have lots of different sizes of bags, boxes, tissue, and bubble wrap."

Sienna grinned. "I've got this. Go wait on your customers."

She spent the rest of the day behind the counter helping and talking with customers and having the best time she'd had in years. She'd been right to come to see Annie. She might not be able to stay, but at least she had been lightened in spirit.

At closing time, Sienna helped Annie close up. Annie led her up a set of back stairs to a living space over the shop—large, light-filled, and open concept. When Annie picked up her phone to make a call, Sienna began to explore the space. There were large windows on the front and both sides. An enormous great room housed distinct areas for living, dining, working and cooking—each blending harmoniously with the rest. The gourmet kitchen was a surprise— Annie had never been much of a cook and absolutely hated it. There was a narrow balcony that stretched across the entire front and could be accessed by two pairs of French doors that flanked the picture window that overlooked the quaint street and charming town.

There was a powder room in the main space, but there was a set of double doors that were thrown open wide, leading to the primary bed and bath. To say it took her breath away was a gross understate- ment. The entire back wall was a set of French doors, flanked by a wall of windows on either side, leading out onto another, grander balcony which overlooked the ocean. The side of the room that had no neighbor was also nothing but windows that looked out into the wilderness and the mountains beyond. On the other side were doors to what she assumed were the primary bath and walk-in closet. Curiously there was little to be found of any furnishings in this space.

Annie joined her out on the back balcony. "Gorgeous, isn't it? The view, I mean."

"Not just the view, but the whole place. It's absolutely spectacular. Can I ask why no bed or dresser?"

Annie nodded. "When Zak returned there was a slight altercation at his welcome home party where I might have had my father with a blade at his throat."

Sienna laughed. "You didn't."

"I did," replied Annie proudly. "Mean old bastard. Anyway, Zak and I agreed it might be better for me to stay with him for a few weeks, so I took some of my stuff out there. I just got off the phone with him to let him know we'll be here for a while. As I recall, you can cook. Why don't we go downstairs and raid the store to find something to make for dinner?"

"Was that salmon somebody brought in to trade?"

"Yes. Wild caught just this morning."

"Good. Let's go get some of that and I'll see what I can't do for side dishes. I saw you had fresh produce."

Annie nodded. "I try to provide local and sustainable products, including food."

They went downstairs and gathered what they needed for an easy pan grilled salmon, buttery sautéed garlic green beans, along with *cacio e pepe*—a simple, quick Italian pasta dish made with just four ingredients.

Annie moaned in delight. "I really had forgotten how well you cook."

"It's nice to cook for someone who wants something other than meat and potatoes."

"I had fun this afternoon. Zak's right; I could use some help, especially if I want to expand."

"Expand?"

"I want to open a little barista/bistro at the side of the store where you're not staring at the side of another building. I'd like to extend the porch and bring it all the way around and have a seating area. Nothing big or fancy, just a place folks can come and get a specialty coffee and maybe a little snack to go with it."

"Mind you, I haven't been here even a day, but from what I saw, I think something like that would go over well."

"I do, too, but we both know I don't cook…"

Sienna laughed. "Yes, I was a bit surprised by how nice and well-equipped this kitchen is."

"I almost opted basically for a kitchenette, but the universe kept telling me to create this awesome, gourmet kitchen."

"It's gorgeous, like everything else. I haven't seen your brother's place, but I can't imagine why you'd agree to move out there."

"There were lots of reasons, but mostly I just needed to be with my big brother. I had a run in with a cave lion a couple of years ago."

"Oh, my god… I thought they were extinct."

"The purebloods are, and the shifters have all but died out. They are loners and mostly have retreated to caves up in frigid places that would make a polar bear think twice."

"You were involved with one?"

"Don't go there. I'm not sure he was involved at all. It was one of my less than brilliant moments, but between that and Old Henry and just missing my big brother, it seemed like the thing to do. I watched you all afternoon. You're great with people, even better than me…"

"I don't know that I'd say that…"

"I would. I know you haven't been here long, and I know you probably feel like your life is in flux, but how about if you agree to stay for a while and help me in the store? I can make part of your compensation living here. If you decide you like it…"

"Where would you stay?"

"Derek, that's my younger brother, and Zak both think it would be better if I stayed close to my big brother. Zak being sheriff will keep Old Henry…" Sienna smiled at the way Annie referred to her sire most often as 'Old Henry' or something more derogatory, "…away from you, but as Zak says an ounce of prevention is worth a pound of cure. Anyway, if you like it well enough to build a new life here, we could talk about creating that bistro and you could run it."

"Even though it would be limited hours and not a

full menu, it would still take a substantial amount of cash."

"I have some money saved that's earmarked for the project, and I could probably borrow the rest."

"Or you could get an investor, someone who's willing to kick in say ten grand for partial ownership in the bistro portion of your business. I could run that when it's open and then help out in the main store the rest of the time."

"You'd do that?" Annie said brightening. "Just like that, you'd throw in with me?"

Sienna grinned and snapped her fingers. "Just like that. My secret dream down in Colorado was to open my own place. I don't have the money to do something like this on my own, although on the drive up here I did start to plan how I could get one of those coffee carts or drive through kiosks, but this would be so much better, especially if we could have a small seating area inside and then out on the deck."

Annie threw her arms around Sienna's neck. "Even better. So, I haven't a clue as to what we need. I just read some articles to get an idea of the cost involved."

"I can start putting together a budget for the actual equipment and set up…"

"And I already have figures for the porch and how to reconfigure the space. Do we need an oven?"

Sienna nodded. "In a perfect world, yes, but we can use the one up here at first. I'm just thinking if we have an oven downstairs, the whole store will smell delicious and we might even be able to do some artisanal breads if you think they'd sell. I saw your cheese selection, it was amazing."

"I think the breads would go big guns. It's hard to find bread to buy here in Otter Cove. Some folks bake their own, thus the reason I have bread machines on display that folks can order, but if we're talking handcrafted bread? I think it could be a real money maker." She laughed. "And one of our biggest customers could be Akiak."

Sienna laughed. "How sweet would that be?"

"You have no idea. We'll need to get you a bed and stuff for the bedroom. Zak and I have been talking about me staying out there on a more permanent basis. I think he'll keep the cottage, and we'll rehab the lower portion of the lighthouse for me. Now to figure out where to put you for tonight…"

"What do you mean? I'll be staying in my gorgeous loft over the store…"

"There's no bed or dressers or…"

"I have three sets of clothes, some extra panties, bras, and socks. And this couch is amazingly comfortable. No, I'm fine right where I am."

"Well, then, partner, there's a bottle of stupidly expensive champagne that I've been saving. Let's crack that sucker open and celebrate. I'll call Zak and ask him to pick me up."

While Annie called Zak, Sienna ran downstairs to

grab some strawberries and chocolate. By the time Annie was finished talking to her brother, Sienna had melted the chocolate, dipped the strawberries in them and set them in the freezer. They opened the champagne and took it, the glasses, and the strawberries out to the balcony off the bedroom where they sat back and talked about the intervening years they'd been apart as the sun's lights faded away.

Sienna raised her glass and toasted Annie. "Here's to the rebirth and renewal of a friendship that meant everything to me, and the launch of a new partnership."

From across the field towards the mountains, a lone figure sat and watched.

CHAPTER 9

SIENNA

The following morning, Sienna woke to a feeling of peace and well-being she hadn't had in a very long time. She wondered if she'd ever had it at all. She'd been up late the night before poring over equipment catalogs and making lists of all the things they'd need.

"Yo, partner!" Annie called as she came up the stairs and walked into the loft. "Yum, what am I smelling?"

"Breakfast. I figured you'd come in early."

"Zak pointed out we should probably put in a door at the top of the stairs."

"We have other things to spend money on—and I have a list."

They ate breakfast at the large kitchen island, and looked at equipment and floor plans of the existing store until it was time to go downstairs and open up.

As they reached the bottom of the stairs, Sienna touched Annie on the shoulder.

"Is there any way we can keep my name off the paperwork, or at least use this name?"

Annie nodded. "Whatever you feel most comfortable with. I think at some point you're going to feel safe enough to be Sienna Carpenter here, but I don't know that I'd ever go back to using Sara MacDonald."

"I have no desire to ever be Sara MacDonald again. Also, do you have a way of getting in touch with the Shadow Sisters?"

"I have access to a drop box chatroom on the dark web. Your paperwork looks really good, and they know what they're doing."

"I'm not worried about me. I'd like to give something back, donate some money or something. I don't know that I'd be alive if it weren't for them. I'd like to help others."

Grinning, Annie said, "You can contribute whatever you want to my monthly donation. If you like, we'll tell them that it's from both of us."

"I should have known you were donating to them."

Backing toward the front door, Annie laughed. "Yeah, you should have." Annie turned toward the door, unlocking it as she called back, "Let's get this party started."

For the rest of the day, the two old friends worked

side-by-side, helping customers and talking about the new bistro. Over and over, they heard that Otter Cove could use something like that and had questions about how soon it would be open.

By the end of the day, Sienna was more exhausted and excited than she'd ever been in her life. She was putting away the last of a delivery of some new goat cheeses when every fiber of her being lit up as though someone had thrown a switch. She whirled around and standing in the doorway into the shop was Zak. Gorgeous, studly, too yummy for words Zak. Zak, her best friend's older brother, the town sheriff and a man who had lived his whole life following and upholding the law.

None of that seemed to matter. Zak was, bar none, the most mesmerizing man she'd ever seen. She could not take her eyes off him. He probably thought she had stalker tendencies, if he'd given her any thought at all.

"Annie went down to the bank. According to her, we had an unusually busy day,"

"I doubt that was a surprise to her. New mystery woman in town? Working in the rogue polar bear girl's shop? People in a place like Otter Cove are bound to want to check it out. And as I'm sure you two were anticipating, word of a new gourmet coffee and pastry shop has spread like wildfire. The café here in town is pretty good, but pretty basic. The idea that there will soon be a place to grab something different or something you can eat on the go has people pretty hyped. That probably sounds pretty pathetic to a city girl like you."

"What makes you think I'm from the city?"

"The clothes you're wearing; the way your hair is cut; everything about you says city."

"Do you always notice things like that? Because you're a cop?"

"Technically, I'm a sheriff, not a cop. I think my training as a SEAL makes me more observant in general, but I would have noticed everything about you if I was blind." Sienna snorted. "Ah. A disbeliever. We'll have to work on that."

Annie chose that minute to return. Sienna wasn't sure if she wanted to hug her or kill her.

"Who's going to work on what?" Annie asked.

"Your friend Sienna and I are going to work on her self-image. She seems to be under the impression that any bear getting a good look at her wouldn't notice everything about her—like her cinnamon-colored hair, those sea-green eyes, the way her curves invite a man to think about all kinds of things he probably shouldn't because she's his little sister's friend and business partner."

"So why are you thinking them?" Annie challenged him.

"You don't know that he is," said Sienna.

Annie and Zak snorted in unison.

"Because at the end of the day, sister mine, I'm an

all-male, alpha bear, and when there's a beautiful woman involved, I notice."

Before Annie could speak again, Sienna pushed past her. "You think I'm beautiful?"

In her whole life, no one had ever told her she was beautiful. If he never spoke another word to her again, she would remember everything about the way he said it: the timbre of his voice, the way the sun shone in and glinted off his hair, the amused and yet sincere look in his eyes.

Annie's more-gorgeous-than-any-man-had-a-right-to-be-brother walked over, placed his finger under her chin, and tilted her head back so she was staring right into his hypnotic eyes. "Yes, little one, I do. And whoever made you doubt that will answer to me if he ever shows his face in Otter Cove."

Sienna wanted to look away; she even tried, but she couldn't. She could hear him speaking, but she was more fascinated by the way his lips moved. She wondered what they might feel like against her own or wrapped around other parts of her feminine body. The idea of Annie's older brother kissing her was one thing; it took her breath away, but the idea of a naked or even semi-naked Zak sucking a pebbled nipple into his mouth or swirling his tongue around her engorged clit before giving it the edge of his teeth made her close her eyes. She stifled a moan and must have looked like her legs were going to buckle as his hand went to her to steady her.

"Easy, Sienna. Annie, didn't you let this poor girl take a lunch break?"

"It's not Annie's fault."

"It isn't?"

"No. It's yours."

"How do you figure that?" he asked, humor crinkling the edges of his eyes and lifting the corners of his mouth.

"Because girls like me don't get hit on by men that look like you."

"I assure you the male bear population of Otter Cove is going to be camping outside your doorstep, and if you cook even half as good as Annie says, you'll be beating them off with a stick. Or better yet, give me a kiss, and I'll do that for you," he said, bestowing the most beautiful smile on her.

She might never have breathed again had Annie not knocked her away from Zak and inserted herself between them. "Knock it off, Zak. Sienna doesn't need you looking at her like you're a starving man and she's porterhouse steak."

He tapped his sister's nose. "I'd rather she was a New York strip. Heavy emphasis on the strip."

"Out!" Annie ordered him in mock severity.

"For now. Are you coming home for dinner?"

"No. I thought we'd go to the café…"

"Or I could cook something here," interrupted Sienna. "Zak could join us if he likes."

The gorgeous mountain of a man with the

brawny shoulders and muscular physique lifted his sister up by her upper arms and set her down so she was no longer between them.

"I would like that very much."

"Do you like scallops?" Sienna asked.

"Who doesn't?" teased Zak.

"We don't have any scallops in today," said Annie.

"That's not a problem. I know Louie Brassard. He's one of the fishermen here in Otter Cove. I'll bet he's got some. How many pounds do you want?"

Sienna grinned at him. Annie's brother was very easy to like. "At least one and a half pounds, two pounds would be even better. Will I need to shuck them?"

"If he doesn't have them already shucked and ready to be delivered some place, I would be surprised. Fresh rather than frozen, right?"

"Scallops do well frozen, but you have to be gentle with how you thaw them."

"I'll let you know what Louie has. It'll take me just a minute." He looked at Annie who was glaring at him. "You be nice." He turned back to Sienna. "And if she says anything mean about me, don't pay her any attention."

"And if she says only good things?"

"Then believe everything that comes out of her mouth."

Before she could stop him; before she could even

realize his intent, he leaned down and brushed his lips against hers before turning and leaving.

Annie closed the door behind her and stared at Sienna, who said, "What? He's just having a little fun at your expense. You should have seen the look on your face."

Annie shook her head. "My brother is one of the finest men you'll ever meet. He's an even better bear-shifter, but you need to understand, if you look up the word brooding or intense in the dictionary, his picture is there. Zak doesn't tease. He doesn't have 'a little fun' at my or anyone else's expense."

"You don't know what you're talking about. Your big brother's picture is in the dictionary beside the word 'gorgeous hunk.'"

"That's two words."

"Whatever. He isn't really interested in me."

"Girl, he's right about one thing. We need to work on your self-esteem."

Annie might have said more, but Zak returned with a bag of shucked and cleaned scallops. "As my lady requested," he said, overly gallant, making Sienna laugh at him.

He might be a big burly hunk of polar bear, but he made her laugh, and he didn't scare her in the least. It was clear Annie adored and respected her brother.

"How do you feel about risotto?" she asked.

"I have no idea what it is, but I'm sure if you're making it, it will be delicious."

Annie groaned. "For god's sake, Zak. You're going to make me puke."

"If you aren't feeling well, little sister, perhaps you should go home and to bed. Sienna and I can have dinner together."

"I feel just fine, big brother, and remember, she was my friend first."

"And if I believe even for a second that I might be the cause of discontent between you two, I'll leave," said Sienna firmly.

"Have I ever mentioned Sienna has a nasty temper?" said Annie brightly.

"Good to know," said Zak before hugging his sister and addressing Sienna. "Nothing could make me turn on my sister or think less of her. Nothing. I don't think she believes that. She's one of the reasons I came home. Something isn't right with her, or with you for that matter, and she won't tell me what it is." The look of shock on Annie's face said Zak had hit the nail on the head. "If she tells you and there's something I can do to fix it, I hope you'll trust me and care enough for my sister to tell me."

"Do you think you can fix the world, Zak?" she asked teasingly, but wondered what his answer might be.

"The world? Probably not. Otter Cove and my clan? Absolutely. I haven't been home long enough to figure out how with as little bloodshed—literally and figuratively—as possible. But know this: I will do whatever it takes to keep you and Annie safe. I'm sheriff here, Sienna. That means something in Otter Cove. And I have the backing of a lot of people here in town. If putting things right means tearing down the walls of Akiak and ousting my father and his cronies and acolytes, I will."

It had suddenly gotten very quiet and still in the room. Not knowing how to respond, Sienna deflected. "I say let's get these scallops cooked right. What are they? I'm not sure I can identify them."

"They're Weathervane scallops. They are a little sweet and buttery with a mild flavor that doesn't stand up to heavy sauces."

Sienna nodded. "I have just the thing: a parmesan and champagne risotto which will use up the champagne we didn't drink last night. It won't take even a half an hour, and I can make us a salad made with romaine and field greens, wild blackberries and a balsamic vinaigrette."

They headed up the stairs into the loft apartment.

"We still need to find her a bed," said Annie.

Her brother looked at her, quirked an eyebrow and said with a perfectly straight face, "Seriously, you're saying that to me? I can think of one she'd fit in nicely."

"And if you aren't careful, Sheriff Grayson, I'm

going to wop you upside the head with my frying pan. You've been warned."

The chuckle that came from low in his throat seemed to dance all over her skin like fireflies in the soft, evening sun, of summer. "I am duly warned, but you should know that here in Otter Cove we take assault on a law enforcement official very seriously."

"What are you going to do, Sheriff? Haul me off to jail in handcuffs?"

"Do you like handcuffs, Sienna? I wouldn't mind seeing you in a set, but it wouldn't be jail I'd haul you off to…"

"You two do know I'm standing here, right? Ick. Now feed me, I'm hungry," said Annie.

"So am I," said Zak in a seductive voice that made Sienna want to shoo Annie out of the loft and find out if he had a set of six or eight-pack abs under his shirt.

"If she doesn't throw cold water on you, big brother, I will."

Sensing there was more disquiet behind her words than he might have initially thought, he hugged Annie close. "Wouldn't do any good, but I'll ratchet it down if that will make you feel better."

"It will."

He looked at Sienna. "But I meant every word I said."

Sienna gulped and could feel the blush rising from her neck and up her cheeks. She must seem like such a country bumpkin to him. Surely, he had figured out she was no city girl.

"I'll get dinner started," she said, turning away.

Zak must have sensed the uneasiness in both of his dining companions, as he seemed to go out of his way to steer the conversation into more neutral territory, telling stories about Annie and Derek, which Annie countered with stories of Zak.

"I honestly don't know when I've had a better meal," said Zak.

"Me, either," said Annie, "and I thought the pasta and salmon from last night would be hard to beat."

"I know you two have your eye on a small bistro with limited hours serving gourmet coffee and pastries, but you might think of offering something a little more robust than that and giving the café a run for its money. That meal was as good as, if not better, than anything I've eaten anywhere in the world."

Annie nodded. "I was thinking the same thing. We were also thinking of making a line of artisanal breads. But one step at a time."

"I understand that, but if at some point you want to expand, I have some money saved up, and I wouldn't mind being a silent investor."

Her face must have had the same stunned expression as Annie's. "Really?"

"Really. You have a true talent, and I think the citizens of Otter Cove would really support a nice place for supper."

"We hadn't thought about anything more grand, but it's worth considering, don't you think?"

Sienna nodded. "I've always wanted a little bistro with a small bakery attached. A whole restaurant is kind of daunting, but in a fun and exciting way."

"Well, I'll leave you ladies to it unless you need me to clean up the kitchen."

"No, we're good," said Annie. "I'll be home in a bit."

"Text me when you're leaving," he said, and Annie groaned. "I know, but it's the big brother in me and I haven't been home for any length of time in over two decades. Indulge me."

"Fine, but at some point, that excuse is going to start to wear thin."

He kissed her on the forehead. "But not tonight."

"But not tonight," Annie agreed.

"I'll let myself out. Sienna, thanks again for the truly outstanding meal."

He headed down the stairs and they heard him lock the door.

"Your brother is nice, but I think he overestimates my appeal on the social scene."

"Do you? Did you not notice how many men came into the store today? Or how many of them were single? And it wasn't just bears. You are like veritable catnip to these guys. Men outnumber women in general in Alaska and in the shifter community the numbers go way up. You're pretty, you're sexy, and you're unattached. He's right about you having to beat them off with a stick when they find out you can cook." Annie turned away, took a couple of steps and then turned back. "Zak wasn't joking. I have known my brother all my life and not once have I seen him act like that. I have never known him to lie or be deliberately cruel. With all of that said, he is a male polar bear—which are not particularly known for their cheery dispositions. Zak is interested in you—as in seriously interested, taking you to mate interested. If you're okay with that…"

"Are you?" Sienna asked, having a hard time accepting that a man with all of Zak's obvious physical characteristics as well as character attributes could be interested in her.

"Me? Absolutely. Zak is a great guy, but if you so much as give him an inch, you'll find yourself mated to him. He won't back off, and he is used to getting what he wants. It's one of the things that made him a highly decorated SEAL. But if you don't want anything to do with him, tell him that now, and I'll back you. If he genuinely believes you have no interest in him, he will probably accept it."

"Only 'probably?'" laughed Sienna.

"Well, he is a dominant alpha male polar bear. They can be a little thick when they think with the head that's between their legs and not the one sitting on top of their necks," said Annie with a grin. Sobering, she said, "He really is a good man and I love him dearly. If I'm right and he's set his sights on you, you could break his heart if you weren't careful. But if you can forget what happened in the past and love my brother—well, nothing would make me happier. Then all I'd have to do is worry about finding a mate for Derek."

"What about you?"

"Me? No way."

"Why not? Wasn't there a guy?"

"We were never meant to be. I didn't believe that at the time, but a lot of people had to get hurt before I understood. But I will never, ever be mated to anyone. Never."

Annie turned her back and Sienna moved closer to console her friend. Annie shrugged out from under her shoulder and then turned back. "Promise me, Sienna. Promise me you won't break Zak's heart."

Sienna nodded. "I promise."

Sienna had a sudden flash of seeing Zak in a kitchen dressed only in jeans that hung low on his hips. Suddenly there was the sound of gunfire and a red hole blossoming with blood on Zak's gorgeous chest as the light flickered out of his eyes. She might be safe with him, but was he safe with her?

CHAPTER 10

ZAK

*Z*ak headed outside and into his truck. The wind shifted ever so slightly and he caught the scent of something he hadn't smelled in a long time. He sniffed the air again and whatever wisp he had caught had faded away. What he thought he smelled wasn't possible. Cave lions had been extinct for thousands of years. But he was certain he had smelled it before and not just in some dream.

He looked up to the second story of Annie's shop where Sienna had taken up residence. Annie thought she needed a bed. Zak knew the bed Sienna belonged in was his, and he meant to see her there before long. That meant he needed to get his sister situated in the lighthouse. He knew from those at Akiak who wanted him to challenge his sire that the old man was spitting nails about the way Annie had managed to get him off balance and in a headlock of sorts with her blade at his throat. He wondered if the old man knew that Annie had not been joking.

Something had happened while he was away. He meant to talk to Derek about it at the earliest opportunity. He was close to both of his siblings, and he'd thought once Annie got used to him being there again that she'd confide in him the way she had when they were kids, but so far, every time he started to probe, she either steered the conversation in a different direction or got angry and stormed off. What the hell was she hiding?

And then there was Sienna. As he recalled, Annie's best friend in college had been her roommate, Sara. Annie had insisted they were different women, but Zak wasn't convinced. He was certain that Sienna meant his sister no harm, but if they were the same woman, why the subterfuge? Why not just admit who she really was?

The most likely scenario was an abusive ex in her past. That would explain a lot of things. Tomorrow he would find a way to get her fingerprints and then run them through a national database via a friend who was still in the service. The guy owed Zak a favor. He would let him know this settled the debt. In order to protect Sienna, he needed to know what he was up against. If it was an ex, Zak would free her of that burden one way or another.

Two women with what he feared were serious, if not deadly, secrets. He needed to figure them out before it exposed them and those around them to danger.

He redirected and focused his thoughts on the construction that he needed to complete on his cottage and the lighthouse where he'd convinced Annie to live. Out there on the point might seem lonely, but he could install an alarm system that would keep them from being vulnerable. And in the lighthouse at least anything or anyone coming for her would have to go through him first.

His cell phone buzzed. "Grayson," he answered.

"Zak, it's Wyatt."

Wyatt was one of the bears in his father's clan who was loyal to him. "He's up to something. He knows her friend is living above the store. I think he might try to take her to leverage Annie into coming home."

"My father has shit for brains. First, I'm the sheriff, and that isn't going to happen. Second, why on earth would he want Annie back at Akiak where she has far more ability to get to him? He can't possibly believe she wouldn't take him out if he pulled that crap with her?"

"You being home has set him off. He's pissed at you for being here and holds you responsible for Derek going to work for Sheriff Miller."

"Jax and I are trying to normalize relations between Mystic River and Otter Cove." He felt like he was an old music CD set on an endless loop.

"There was a time when, as the two largest shifter communities in Alaska, the towns worked together. Now it feels a bit like we're sitting on a lit powder keg, and neither Jax nor I know how long the fuse is."

Zak slowed his SUV and found a place wide enough to make a sharp U-turn.

"I hate to be a pain in the butt, but it would go a long way to settling things down in Otter Cove if you'd oust your father and claim leadership. I believe you have far more support than you think you do. But that's a discussion for another day. Two SUVs just pulled away from the house. I'll try to see where they're headed."

"If you got those trackers planted on all the clan's vehicles, I'll be able to locate them. In the interim, I'm headed back into town. I think Annie and Sienna would be better off out at the lighthouse with me."

"I wouldn't disagree with that assessment. Call if you need help. If I don't hear from you within the hour, I'll come to you with reinforcements."

"Good. I'll be at the store, the lighthouse cottage, or the main road in between."

"Talk to you in sixty minutes."

Zak picked up his speed. Wyatt might well be a pain in the butt, but he was a pain in the butt with good instincts. Realizing his tablet was back at the cottage and his laptop was in his office, he cursed to himself, as those were the devices on which he had installed the tracking app.

Damn it.

He realized for the first time in a long time that the she-bear he was most concerned about was not his sister. It was Sienna—his fated mate.

Whoa. Where had that thought come from? He realized he wasn't questioning whether or not it was true, but only when the realization had taken root in his bones that she was. It certainly explained the murderous rage he'd had to fight down all day each time some male bear had come anywhere close to her. He would need to make sure that the word got spread around that the new, pretty cinnamon bear-shifter was off limits.

Cinnamon bear? How stupid can I be? How did I not recognize Sienna as my fated mate? Was she as unaware as she appeared to be?

The need to return to town and ensure both his mate and his sister were safe was almost overwhelming. There was something wrong. He could feel it in his bones. He called Wyatt.

"Zak?"

"How easily could you and five or six of our men get into town?"

"Trouble?"

"That I can tell you what and where it is? No. I only have my cell phone with me and didn't bother downloading the tracking app on it. A problem I will remedy as soon as possible. I just don't want you guys thirty minutes out if there's trouble."

"Got it. We're on it and will be headed your way in less than five."

Zak could hear him scrambling, and quietly calling some of the others. "Make sure those with you know the score and that the others know to remain at Akiak until they hear otherwise. One of you needs to split off and get into my office. The door code is 1-2-3-4. I know, not very original, but I haven't changed it yet. There is no security code on my laptop. Open the app and see where they are. The rest need to head to Annie's mercantile. Move in quietly, and if you don't see anything, remain out of sight."

"Got it."

Zak could feel adrenaline flowing through his veins. The same kind of heated rush that existed before a battle. Only this time, the stakes were higher than they'd ever been. If Henry was as pissed as Wyatt had reported, he might well be willing to inflict serious injury on Sienna to get Annie's cooperation. Zak knew, although not from Annie, that the old man had done it before. Wyatt and the others might be right, the time may have come to move against Henry. The problem was he now wanted time to secure and claim his mate. Then he would make his move, but only after he had Annie and Sienna safe in Mystic River with Derek.

There were probably those who still believed Derek was the same surly screw-up he'd always been. Zak knew different. The fight with Jax last year had made him grow up and face a few unpleasant truths about himself. Many a long-distance video call, private message, and email had convinced Zak that Derek was finally maturing into a man he was proud to call brother.

He initiated a call. "Zak?" his brother answered. "Trouble?"

"Not sure. I need you to get a boat and head to the lighthouse."

"What's going on?"

"Not sure, but everything in me tells me Annie and my fated mate might be in danger."

"Fated mate? What fated mate? How could you hold out on me?"

"I just realized it this evening. She's a friend of Annie's. One of my people up at Akiak said the old man and some of his thugs were on the move."

"He'll be after Annie."

"That's what I'm thinking and won't think twice about using Sienna against her."

"Why don't I meet you in town?"

"No, I've got some of my people headed there now. I think we can handle Henry and his goon squad, but I want to be able to put both of them out of danger. Move Derek. I need your help."

"I'm headed out the door."

Zak ended the call and hurried into the night. If Henry so much as mussed a hair on either Sienna or Annie's heads, he'd slash open his fucking chest and rip out his beating heart. The streetlights that lined Main Street were up ahead. Choosing stealth over speed, he parked his car in a secluded spot in one of the alleys close to Annie's, grabbed his rifle from the rack in the SUV and started to make his way toward the mercantile. At the end of the alley, Zak had planned to ensure no one was close and to sneak around the corner in order to get to Annie's.

No such luck. He could smell the cigarettes and the musk of polar bears along with hearing the men joking and talking. He would have court martialed any man under his command for doing the same. Unfortunately, he was no longer in the Navy and these yahoos didn't work for him. Still a direct confrontation might do more good than harm. If they didn't stand down, he'd slit their throats and have two less to deal with. Shouldering his rifle in a way that he could bring it into position to fire if necessary, he readied his knife at his back and stepped out into the light.

CHAPTER 11

SIENNA

From the moment she arrived, Sienna had found an easy rhythm to working with Annie. Once Sienna entered the store, it was as if the time apart had never been lost and their friendship had renewed and evolved and an organic kind of synergy had blossomed between them.

"Do you think Zak was serious about investing in a restaurant with us?"

Annie finished drying the pot in which Sienna had made the risotto—a heavy-bottomed, straight-sided skillet—and turned to her. "I do. I know for the past twenty years he's lived very simply and lived in base-supplied housing, so I suspect he has a shit-ton of cash. When I broke away from Old Henry, Zak offered to invest in the store, but at the time it was important to me to do things on my own."

"I can understand that. I think there are times we

are ready and willing to accept help from others and times we are not. I think the important thing is to recognize both."

"Agreed. So, what do you think?"

"You're asking me?"

"I am. I don't just want an employee. I want a partner."

"But you've done so much work…"

"And you know the barista market and what that should look like. I say we play to each other's strengths. We both know I can't cook. I've known since we were at the university you could bake. What you've proved the last two nights is that you can cook. Seriously, those were the best two dinners I've had in forever. I only told people about my idea for a bistro with gourmet coffees and some snacks, but honestly, I've always wondered about having a more upscale kind of place. But I want to see if we can make a go of the coffee shop first."

Sienna nodded. "I know you were thinking about the bistro being open ten to two, but I think we'll miss a lot of business if we aren't open early—maybe make it seven to two. Then if we want to open a restaurant, we can expand. I think if we do, we might have to reconfigure things, but we can buy baking equipment that will allow for our expansion."

"Now you're talking. Before I knew you'd be here, I'd been dreading going to Anchorage to look for ovens and that kind of thing."

"I know it's expensive to bring stuff up from Seattle or Canada, but honestly, I think we can find better deals, even with the cost of shipping it up here."

"And we may be able to make a deal on that by using a couple of locals I know and not one of the big importers."

"Is there some kind of storage space in town?"

"Why do you ask?"

"Because if you're going further than Anchorage, it might do to look to see if there are deals to be made —things like a restaurant or bakery or barista going out of business."

"I think it makes more sense for you to go, but I also can see why you might not want to."

"I have spent the past several years being afraid. I'm done with that. I don't want to be the kind of person whom fear was causing me to become. Besides, can one of the guys we'd use to bring stuff up here give me a ride down and bring stuff back?"

"Yeah," said Annie nodding, "I think we can make that work."

"Then I'll head down to Seattle. I think that's the place we're most likely to find something."

"When?"

"The sooner the better as far as I'm concerned."

The words were barely out of Sienna's mouth when the front doors into the store below rattled as something large hit them and they held.

"What the hell was that?" cried Sienna.

"Nothing good," replied Annie, reaching for her cell phone. "Next thing we do is get a proper door at the top of the stairs and a better alarm system."

The doors banged and rattled again as Annie dialed Zak, Sienna assumed. "Shit," said Annie. "It went directly to voicemail."

The third time someone tried to force the doors, they gave way, and the alarm did go off, but the sound of several people running was easily heard.

"They're headed to the stairs," said Annie, grabbing Sienna by the hand and leading her towards the bedroom.

They locked the doors as they heard heavy footfalls coming up the stairs. The two women dashed into the bath and closed and locked its doors, as well. They could hear two or more people rumbling around in the main living area, knocking things over and snarling.

"They aren't bears, are they?" asked Sienna.

"My guess is my father. I made a fool of him when Zak came home. I'm not surprised he's retaliating. They're not shifted, and the alarm should bring people, but you need to get out of here. Old Henry won't think twice about turning you over to your old clan. You go out the window and go for Zak. Take the first right as you head back…"

"I'm not leaving you."

"You have to. We're going to need Zak. He'll

probably know about the alarm and be headed back, but we need to make sure. Old Henry won't hurt me, but I can't guarantee…"

Both women screamed and held each other tight as something heavy hit the door, and the loud angry roar of a bear could be heard. Another heavy thump and another growl preceded the sound of rolling thunder combined with the hiss of electrical power.

"Sienna? Annie?"

"We're here, Zak," said Annie as she and Sienna released the tight hold they'd had on each other.

Annie moved on unsteady legs and unlocked the door. Zak stepped through and hugged his sister close. When he opened his arm to include Sienna, she flew into his embrace as though it was the easiest thing she'd ever done. The moment his arm closed around her, the thought that kept repeating in her head was 'home.'

"You two okay?" he asked.

"Did that bastard break my doors?" snarled Annie as she squirmed out of Zak's arms and exited the bath.

An audible grunt and groan could be heard as Annie kicked the bear her brother had taken down.

"That's going to leave a mark," teased Zak. "But you're both okay, right?"

Sienna nodded and realized she was still hugging Zak tightly. The poor man probably couldn't breathe, not to mention he probably didn't need his sister's friend squishing him. She tried to wriggle away, but Zak refused to relinquish his hold.

"You're fine where you are," he rumbled in a kind of contented way.

There was something fine about being held by Zak Grayson. Fine until she realized that his big, hard, naked cock was throbbing between them. By the way it felt, it was enormous. She thought about taking a peek but thought that might be rude. Besides which, she might have to move away from him, and that really wasn't something she wanted to do.

She knew that when shifters shifted back to their human form, they were rendered naked. Nudity, in and of itself, didn't bother her. And she didn't mind Zak's at all. It felt good to be held in strong arms. She was balanced against him, his arms around her holding her tight to his body.

"Do you know who they were?" she asked as she heard someone dragging something heavy, presumably the same guy Annie had kicked away.

"Two of them I recognize, but all of them were from Akiak. My guess is they were after Annie."

Sienna nodded, her hair moving up and down his chest. "She said she'd made your sire look like a fool."

Zak chuckled. He had a marvelous chuckle—deep, sensual, and inclusive in a way that made you want to laugh with him, even if you didn't understand the joke.

"That would be putting it mildly. He crashed a

welcome home party for me, and two of his goons
rushed Derek—that's our younger brother—and me.
Annie slipped by them and held the old man at knife
point. There wasn't anyone there, including Henry
himself, who wasn't absolutely certain that she'd have
slit his throat."

"She hates him…"

"You haven't met him. Once you do, you'll understand why. I probably shouldn't have left and gone
into the Navy, but I wasn't ready to take the old
bastard on back then."

"And now?"

"And now I believe it's inevitable. There's a schism
developing within the clan, which doesn't bode well
for any of us, but the numbers of Henry's supporters
are starting to dwindle. I'll need to provide a place for
those who came tonight. They sure as hell can't go
back to Akiak."

A man Sienna had never seen before stuck his
head inside the door. "Zak, we got all the ones that
were here at the building. Should we take them to the
jail?"

"Absolutely. I'll come down and do the actual
processing. How many?"

"I saw two vehicles leave the compound. Henry
was in one of them, and we haven't seen him or the
other vehicle."

"Get someone up at Akiak to get any family you
have up there out and down here. I'll wake up the

hotel and we can take it over. I think keeping everyone in one place where we can have a guard is what I want."

"I was careful. None of us that came tonight have anything or anyone back at Akiak."

"Good enough. Call…"

"I think we'd be better out at your place. We can grab some camping gear for tonight. That way we're all together."

Zak turned to look at the tall, brawny blond, "What about Cicely?"

The man grinned. "Waiting in the SUV. Cicely is my mate," he said to Sienna. "I'm Wyatt, by the way. Zak, do you want me to get you something to wear, or are you good just standing there naked, holding that gorgeous woman in your arms?"

"I was fine until you brought it to her attention."

"He didn't. Trust me, I'd noticed."

"You keep your eyes up here."

"Why? The view is better south of your eyes—sculpted pecs, washboard abs, and that rather impressive cock—although I must say, you have the most amazing eyes ."

Zak laughed out loud; Wyatt joined him.

"Annie, Cicely, and now this one?" said Wyatt. "I'm not sure that is a triumvirate we want to deal with."

"No choice in the matter." Zak looked down at her. "Wyatt is, or will be, my second in command.

He's good at logistics. There was many a time I cursed the day he left the SEALs and came back up here to take Cicely to mate. Wyatt, get the downstairs secured. Derek should already be at my place. Get a couple of our guys out there to back him up. You and Cicely can use my bed; Annie can stay in hers. Derek should be there by now, and he and any of our men that need to can stay in the lighthouse tonight. Grab what we need in terms of camping equipment."

It was easy to picture Zak as a commander and a SEAL and even easier to tell Wyatt was used to following Zak's orders. "Leave two of the men here in town. They can stay with the prisoners in the jail tonight."

"Got it," said Wyatt.

"Annie is not to be left alone even for a minute."

"You worried about them coming after her again, or her going after them?" quipped Wyatt.

"With my little sister, either one is possible. But she's to be under close guard. In the morning, assess what we're going to need to make the lighthouse more defendable and comfortable for the men. Then head up here and we can come up with a plan. Sienna, can I count on you to get something pulled together for breakfast?"

"Absolutely. How many people are we talking about?"

"Eleven, including you and Derek."

"That won't be a problem. Should I worry about the prisoners?"

"No. Henry's goons decide they want to start a war, they can bloody well starve for all I care."

She grinned. "What time?"

"Can we do seven? That'll give us time to formulate a plan of action and get everyone moving on it."

"Absolutely. Are you staying out with your men in the jail?"

Wyatt chuckled. "And with that I am off to execute our fearless leader's orders." Wyatt ducked out, and she could hear him laughing all the way down the stairs.

"Why is he laughing?"

"While the doors downstairs have been closed up, and I doubt we'll have any more problems, you, like my little sister and Cicely, for that matter, will all be closely guarded. Henry is not above using you and Cicely to force my sister's hand. I'll be staying here with you."

"Oh." She cast her glance around the sparse area. "I know I don't have a bed yet, but the only thing suitable to sleep on is the couch. That's not big enough for you."

"I suppose I'd be pushing my luck if I told you it would be plenty big enough if we were curled up together."

Sienna could feel the heat rising in her cheeks. She hadn't blushed in years, and yet around Zak she was easily flustered. She wasn't sure what to say. Surely, he was just teasing her so she'd forget about how bad things could have been, wasn't he? Annie couldn't possibly be right about Zak. He was so far out of her league.

Her thought was interrupted when his hand connected with her backside with a sharp smack that sent heat, followed by pain, flashing across it.

"I wouldn't like what just went through your head, now would I?" he growled in a voice that made her shiver.

"Um, probably not."

His hand flashed again, but this time remained resting on the spot he'd swatted as if to hold the heat in. "Then I suggest you don't think that way anymore. Understood?"

"Um, yes, but that still doesn't solve the problem of where you're sleeping."

"I didn't think you'd go for sharing the couch. I'll grab what I need from downstairs and sleep on the floor."

"That doesn't seem fair. I suppose if we each put our heads down at one end, we can find a way to fit."

Zak shook his head, tilting her chin up so that she was caught by his entrancing eyes. "Pay attention, Sienna. If I share the couch with you, I'm not going to need clothes, and neither will you. If I share the couch with you, we'll be doing a lot more than sleeping."

CHAPTER 12

ZAK

*T*here, he'd said it. Although the hard cock that still throbbed between them should have made that clear without the words. He wondered what she'd been told, by whom, and for how long that made her doubt her innate beauty and sensuality. He hadn't been kidding when he'd said they were going to need to work on that. But they had time—all the time in the world. He meant to spend the rest of his days making her happy and seeing that she believed she was everything to him.

And if she even had a clue as to what he was thinking she'd run like hell, and that he couldn't allow. If she forced his hand, he was going to need to deal with Annie. He shouldn't have to; she should have long since been mated. Derek had mentioned something about Annie and some guy, but she'd returned home, packed, and left Akiak. He would need to find out what the hell was going on with her.

But at the moment, he needed to deal with his fated mate. The fact that she didn't know she was his fated mate was, as far as Zak was concerned, sort of beside the point.

"Wha… what do you mean?" Sienna asked.

"I think you know what I mean, but just in case you don't, I'll spell it out for you. Your choice is either sleeping on that couch all by yourself with me on the floor, or sharing that couch with me, in which case we will be having sex all night."

Not the most seductive or gentle way to tell her what he wanted, but he'd had a hard-on from the time Annie had wriggled free until now.

"You… you want to have sex with me?"

"I would think that is painfully obvious."

Sienna pushed away from him. "That's not a good idea, Zak."

He took a step back to give her space but leaned against the vanity with his legs stretched out, preventing her from leaving easily. "Why not?"

"Well, for one thing you're Annie's brother…"

"I'm pretty damn sure Annie would be very supportive of a bonding between the two of us. You're her good friend, and I'm the older brother she adores. Next?"

"We've only just met; we don't know each other."

"Immaterial. Our kind—bear-shifters—have been

recognizing our fated mates…" Now, that was out there, too. "… for as long as our kind have been around. I don't know all the rules cinnamon bears have about these things, but polar bears, because of our harsh environment, tend not to spend a lot of time in long, drawn-out courtship rituals. My sister tells me we're far more neanderthal up here than down in the lower forty-eight."

"You just put it right out there, don't you?" she said, her body losing all the languidity it had before.

"I believe in talking straight with people. You ask me a question; I'll answer it or tell you I'm not going to answer it."

"I'm not your fated mate."

"Says who?"

"Says me."

Now, she was becoming belligerent.

"That might work for you, but it doesn't for me. I was forced…" she seemed to stop herself from completing the sentence.

"Forced to what? And more importantly by whom?"

"It isn't important."

"It is to me. I need to know if I need to worry about any threat other than Henry. And for the record, the idea of anyone, other than me, forcing you to do anything makes my blood boil. I will tell you for a fact that if anyone, again, other than me, lays one finger on you without an invitation from you, I'll tear

the bastard limb from limb. Polar bears may be somewhat cave-like but we take the protection of our mates
seriously."

"I'm not a polar bear," she said, crossing her arms
over her chest, which might have proved far less
adorable if they hadn't been perched on top of her
ample breasts. God, the girl had a great set of tits. He
couldn't wait to get his hands on them—or better yet,
his mouth.

Might as well put it out there so she could get used
to the idea. "You will be once I claim you."

Her eyes widened and then narrowed. He'd pissed
her off. Even though they weren't pair bonded, he
could feel the wave of anger rolling off her.

"Claim me? Your egotistical jerk. You may be
God's gift to the world to look at, but no one, and I
mean no one is ever going to force me to do anything
I don't want to do." She stepped forward and poked
him in the chest. Apparently, the truth about the
danger in poking a bear had never been explained to
her. "Got that?"

"Has anyone ever told you, you're even more
beautiful when you're angry?"

"No one has ever told me I was beautiful, so they
can't have told me I was more beautiful when I'm
pissed."

He chuckled. "I'll have to see about fixing that."

She stomped her foot and growled at him. She
must sense that she had no need to fear him. She-

bears could be a cantankerous lot, and corporal punishment was often used to keep them in line. Zak had found most females could benefit from a swift swat to their backsides—certainly she had seemed to have softened after the first one, but he'd need to be careful that she never felt abused.

"You are incorrigible," she snorted—even that was adorable.

"Absolutely. Now am I having sex with you or sleeping on the floor?"

"Neither. You're going to get out of here and leave me alone."

"That, my sweet cinnamon bear, is not going to happen."

"Want to bet?" she snarled.

"Every last dime I have." He'd let the matter ride for now. "I'm going to assume that I have yet to seduce or persuade you with my charming manners and masculine perfection—although I do think you noticed the latter. By the way, unless you're planning to make use of my cock, quit looking at it. You're giving it all kinds of mixed messages, and it's getting frustrated and annoyed."

"What about the rest of you?" she said, trying, he could tell, to keep from grinning at him.

Poor girl, he almost felt sorry for her. She could feel the pull of being his fated mate even if she didn't want to or perhaps didn't recognize it for what it was.

"The rest of me is far more civilized and patient. I'll just tell my cock that it has to be the same."

"Do you think it'll listen?"

"Probably. It won't like it, and it'll give me hell, but in the end it'll have to just dream of what it's going to be like to be up inside you, feeling your pussy pulse all around it."

Sienna rolled her eyes as she shook her head. "I'm not sure you and your dick have evolved enough to be a neanderthal." She took a deep breath. "Look, I'm really tired, and I want to go to bed."

"Good. Let's get you naked, too, and I can show you just how cozy that couch can be."

"Does your sister know what an asshole you can be?"

"I'm afraid she does." He grew serious. "Unless I miss my guess, Annie has already warned you that she didn't think I was teasing at dinner. In case you didn't believe her, I wasn't. You are my fated mate, Sienna Carpenter. Whatever or whoever you're running from…"

"Who says I'm running?"

"Everything about you says you are. Whoever it is will not take you away from me. Never doubt that you are my fated mate or that I will protect you with everything I have until I draw my last breath. I am mindful that we haven't known each other long, but you know that I speak the truth."

"God, what is it about male bears that you just believe you can subjugate us?"

"Us as in she- bears?" She nodded and he sucked his lower lip between his teeth, thinking. "Thousands of years of precedence on our side. And I have no intention of subjecting you to anything bad. Will I expect a certain level of obedience, especially in front of others? Yes. Will I discipline you if I don't get it? Probably. But I will also never abuse you. I will not make decisions in a vacuum. I will solicit your input. I may not, in the end, do what you want me to do, but I will listen to what you have to say, and it will weigh in my decision."

"And what? I'm just supposed to strip naked, get down on the floor and offer myself to you?"

"That would make my cock happier than it's ever been, but my guess is that's not going to happen, so I'll go downstairs and get some things to make up a bed on the floor." He drew himself up off the vanity and headed for the door.

"Zak? Do you think they'll come back?"

"Tonight? Doubtful. Sometime in the future? Most definitely. This was Henry's opening salvo in the fight he wants to bring to me, Annie, and Derek."

"Then shouldn't Derek be here?"

"No. Derek is still too much of a hothead and too easily baited into a fight. Henry's fight has to be with me. He's figured out I'm not ready to have that fight, so if he can use you, Annie, or Derek to provoke me before I'm ready, he has a better chance of besting me."

"Can he beat you?"

"As in win? No. I have far more supporters within the clan than he believes. And while he might be willing to send his goons to maim or even kill me, I very much doubt he has the stomach to do it himself. I know for a fact he doesn't have the skill. That's the difference between us—I have no such qualms. If it comes to it, I'll challenge him to a fight to the death, and I'll win, and then I'll never think of him again."

He worried for a moment that he'd been too frank, had shown her the primal part of himself he had never shared with anyone before. But then he saw the fire in her eyes. There was a primal part of his mate that responded to the feral nature of the beast within.

"Good. I may not be your fated mate…"

"But you are."

"Regardless. I wouldn't want to see you killed."

He stepped towards her, trapping her against the shower when she backed away. "Never fear, my little cinnamon bear, you won't. I came home knowing I had a fight ahead of me and that there was something more that awaited me."

He stroked her hair away from her face as he leaned down to press a gentle kiss against her lips. Zak deepened the kiss as his tongue slipped past her lips to tangle with hers, and she moaned as she opened her mouth to him. The first tentative probe of her tongue into his mouth made his cock jump between them. He wanted all of her as much as his dick wanted her pussy, but his dick was going to have to wait.

His little cinnamon bear needed time, tenderness, and affection. Right now, he could give her all three. Depending on what she was running away from, that might change in the future, but he would give her as much as he could. And sex—his cock screamed—and sex. His cock could be a real jerk when it wanted to be. He reassured it. The rest of him wanted sex just as bad, which was curious as in the past it had only been his cock wanting to feel the snug fit of a woman's pussy as it slid in and out. It was a biological imperative he gave into on a regular basis.

But with Sienna, it was so much more than that. He could smell her arousal as he pressed her against the glass of the shower door, drawing out the amount of time he could stay close. God, she was sweet.

Tonight, though, he needed answers—not necessarily from her, although if she offered, he certainly wasn't going to turn her down. No, he needed answers about Henry's movements, which would help them figure out what the old bastard was up to.

CHAPTER 13

SIENNA

*S*ienna was certain she would never understand men or male bears, specifically the alpha ones. Zak had ended the kiss and then left her to go downstairs to get a pillow, an air mattress, a sleeping bag, and a pair of jeans. Upon returning, other than to tease her that if she changed her mind all she had to do was call his name, he'd crawled into the sleeping bag and fallen asleep.

He would never know what it had cost her not to give into the fire he'd lit within her with his kiss. She'd been kissed before, although Kurt's idea of foreplay was to force her to suck his cock until either he shoved deep and streamed his semen into her throat or brought her up and told her to turn around so he didn't have to look at her face while he bred her.

No doubt, Zak wanted the same thing from her— to take his pleasure—but she sensed in him that it would be an exchange of pleasure and that he would ensure she got more than she had to give. She used to read about that kind of thing in romance books, but when it became clear that she would never have that kind of connection or even physical pleasure with Kurt, she'd found the books too distressing and had taken to reading thrillers—usually those involving serial killers. Sienna wasn't sure what that said about her, but she was sure it wasn't good.

She lay on her side and watched him sleep. She had to stay awake because every time she closed her eyes, all she could see was his naked body with its broad shoulders, cut chest, sculpted abs, and sexy hip notches which pointed straight to his enormous cock. She wasn't sure if the damn thing would even fit, but she knew she wanted to try.

Sienna was miserable as she lay on her back on the couch. Her nipples were so hard they ached, and she wondered if that was what it was like for him having his cock hard like that. Her pussy was soft and wet. She felt things for and about Zak that she had never, ever felt for anyone before, and certainly not for Kurt. For the briefest moment she inhaled deeply, scenting his musk and making everything even worse.

What would it be like to be mated to a bear like Zak? Would he really be a mate who would listen to her and not just slap her and tell her to shut up when she dared to offer an opinion that differed from his? What would it be like to have someone she could share her life with and dive into together? What if it could be like in romance novels, and end with a happily ever after and not counting up the dead bodies?

She was unlikely to ever know. Maybe it wasn't safe for her at all, but the idea gutted her. How could she have become so attached to a place in such a short amount of time? She had known it would be good to see Annie, but how was she to know that somehow, inextricably Annie's older brother was her fated mate? Oh, she knew that's who he was, had known from the moment he scooped her up off the ground, but she hadn't allowed herself to believe it.

When he'd blatantly stated earlier that he would kill for her, a kind of visceral thrill had gone through her. Not that she wanted to see anyone dead, although seeing Kurt put in a hospital wouldn't hurt her feelings, but just to know she mattered enough to someone that they would risk injury had given her a feeling of peace. But would she want Zak to risk himself that way? Would it be a risk? As far as she knew, no one in her origin clan had ever seen combat, much less been a commando, and Annie had indicated a great many of those up at Akiak had been SEALs or Rangers.

It took very little for her to imagine how those large, calloused hands would feel running over her skin, holding her close as he drove that magnificent staff of his into her over and over again. She could dream about the way the hair on his chest would brush her nipples as he moved over and inside her. It was the reason she didn't dare close her eyes and why she gripped the bedclothes on the couch so tightly. The last thing she needed was for him to catch her masturbating or fantasizing about him.

No, dawn couldn't come too quickly. She rose before he did, moving quietly into the kitchen to begin to get things ready to make food. She heard him stir and purposely turned her back, she didn't need to see him get out of that sleeping bag naked—didn't need to see him doing anything naked. Zak being naked was already an image that was burned into her brain.

"Good morning, gorgeous," he said wrapping his arms around her and nuzzling the side of her neck.

"Don't do that," she said, turning within the circle of his arms, which brought her face to his chest and her sex into contact with his cock. Granted that hard length was encased in his jeans, but that did little to affect her reaction to him.

"Hmm," he all but purred. "I like this much better." He lowered his head to hers, and swallowed her protest, kissing her deeply until she stopped struggling and allowed herself the brief luxury of allowing herself to believe.

"You don't fight fair, and you are way too quiet."

He chuckled, the deep amused rumble that she swore she could feel as well as hear. "I'm a SEAL—moving quietly is often the difference between living and dying. As for fighting fair, that's not true. But keep in mind, all is fair in love and war."

"Zak, don't. I need to get this food made, or your men will go hungry."

"For now," he said, taking a step back. "But there's going to come a time I'm going to want you to fix my breakfast wearing nothing more than a flimsy apron."

She laughed. "Why bother with that?"

"Because I like bacon, and hot bacon grease spattering on your chest hurts. Trust me, I speak from experience."

Why couldn't she actually dislike him the way she wanted him to believe she did? Things would be so much easier and so much less complicated.

"You do know you're impossible, right?"

"I'm afraid he doesn't know that at all," said a man from behind him who could only be Zak's younger brother, Derek.

Zak growled.

Derek laughed. "Annie wasn't kidding. You do have it bad. For the record, Sienna, he's never been that easy to bait before."

"And did Annie warn you I'd reach down your throat and rip your liver out if you don't stop making googly eyes at my mate?"

"I do believe she did say something along those lines. Look, I can't stay for breakfast, although by the smell of things, I'm wishing I could. I spoke to Jax.

He said to let you know we have people to back whatever play you want to make."

"Thanks, Derek."

"No apology for the growl or the threat?" Sienna asked.

"None, because he meant both. I can't decide whether to be a good brother and tell you to give him a break and take it easy on him or tell you to make his life a living hell so I can sit back and watch."

"Welcome to the Bickering Grayson Brothers' show," said Annie as she crested the stairs, followed by one of the men Sienna recognized from last night. "Would you please tell this jerk that if he runs into me one more time because I stopped short, I'm going to rip his balls off?"

"No," said Zak evenly. "I will not tell him that, and you will not rip his, or anyone else on our side's, balls off. And if I catch you close enough to do it to someone from the other side, I'll put you somewhere you can't see daylight until this is over." He turned to look at Sienna. "That goes for you, as well."

"Annie, have I mentioned your brother is a jerk?"

"If you only think he's a jerk, he's been on his best behavior…"

"Or she hasn't been paying attention, but given the fact that Zak is half naked, I doubt that's the case. Even old mated she-bears like me notice when Zak the Magnificent is walking around shirtless." The last bit ended with a squeak as Wyatt popped Cicely's backside. Instead of being angry, she turned and wrapped her arms around his neck. "But my heart, soul, and a bunch of other body parts belong only to you, my beloved mate."

Wyatt chuckled. "It's a good thing you spent a lot of time last night proving that to me, you wicked little minx." He gave her a quick kiss. "In case you missed it, Sienna, this wanton creature in my arms is my mate, Cicely."

"Anything I can do to help? We all know Annie can't cook, and there are a bunch of hungry bears on the way in."

Cicely moved toward the kitchen and between the two of them they managed to put together a hearty breakfast for all. After breakfast, the men cleared a space to lay a set of blueprints, brought out a white board, and began to plan the best way to get their people out of Akiak.

Annie and Sienna went downstairs to open the store, grateful to Cicely who had assured them she'd get the kitchen in tip top shape.

"You made him sleep on the floor in a sleeping bag in front of the stairs? Good for you."

"I doubt there is little anyone could make your brother do if he wasn't already so inclined. I did not give in to my baser nature and have sex with him, but sleeping in front of the stairs was his idea."

Annie nodded. "Trust me, you'll have a proper

door there by nightfall. So, you wanted to have sex with my big brother."

"Yes, I did. God, why did you never tell me he was such a hunk?"

"Because I'm his sister and hunk does not equal big brother. Look, I don't want to make this difficult, but keeping secrets from Zak isn't going to work. You need to tell him. He can help. He's Otter Cove's sheriff; he's a former SEAL; he's about to become alpha to the clan; and he's an all-around badass. Zak hates secrets. Being a SEAL, having his team betrayed, his history with my stepmother—all of that left him wary and suspicious. If he hasn't already told you, he has strong feelings for you. He truly believes you are his fated mate." Sienna said nothing and just lowered her eyes. She couldn't allow Annie to see the truth that lay there. Not yet. "Oh, my god, he's right. You can feel it, too. Okay, now you're lying to him, and he can be a ruthless bastard when someone's lying."

"I'm not lying. I just don't know how I feel about it or what I want to do about it. I'm not about to get passed around like some football trophy, and he doesn't need more trouble brought to his doorstep. Besides, this is moving way too fast for me."

"I get it. You'd probably like a little bit of time between getting out of one lousy, horrible, awful relationship and into one with a bear who will love you like no other, will never hurt you, and will ensure you're happy for the rest of your days. I totally understand you not wanting to rush in." Annie shook her by her shoulders. "What are you, nuts?"

"Well, when you say it like that. Do you mind if I go for a quick walk down on the beach? I love being this close to the ocean. I never thought I'd live anywhere that wasn't landlocked."

"I guess, but make it quick. The guys all seem to think Old Henry is back at Akiak licking his wounds, but you can never be too careful. Besides, if something happens to you, I'm not sure Zak would ever forgive me."

Sienna squeezed her arm. "I'll be fine. I may not be a polar bear, but I am a she-bear and one who is kind of done with having any man—regardless of how sexy he is—telling her what to do."

"For what it's worth. I think you and Zak are going to get along fine. And I am going to love having you for a sister." Annie fished out a semi-automatic pistol.

"I don't think…"

"I don't care. Henry is dangerous. So is your ex, from what you've said. I understand the need to be alone for a few minutes. Zak and the rest of them can be a bit overwhelming. Take it. You do know how to use it, right?"

"I'm from Colorado. Of course, I know how." While technically true, Sienna had always hated guns, so while she knew how to shoot one, she wasn't a very good shot.

Sienna turned from the house and made her way down to the beach via the winding path down the rocky cliff. She squatted down, scooped up some of the fine sand in her hand and then stood, letting it trickle out of her fingers.

"Leave it to you to find a place colder than Colorado," said a voice she'd truly never thought she'd hear again.

She turned around, fear settling like a cannon ball in her belly as her eyes confirmed what her ears had told her to be true.

Kurt.

CHAPTER 14

SIENNA

There was no way he could have found her. She'd done everything the Shadow Sisters had told her. She hadn't even used any of the credit cards they'd given her. She'd doubled back, paid cash and changed cell phones. How had he found her?

"What's the matter, bitch? Not expecting to see me? Did you really think you could escape me? Give me that," he said, grabbing the gun away from her.

"Go away, Kurt. You never wanted me."

"I can't let my father and the others think you were able to outsmart me."

"No, but you could tell them you caught up with me and killed me to free yourself of the burden of being mated to me. After all, I'm barren, and you want sons."

She could see that he was considering his options. She was also sure that he saw actually killing her as one of those options. Given he had the gun, Sienna was fairly sure it would occur to him, and he might consider that his best option. Spinning on her heel, she began to run. She thought about heading back to the store, but feared with a gun he might hurt or kill people who didn't deserve to be drawn into this drama.

Sienna heard the shot before the sand off to the side spat as the bullet hit. Kurt wasn't much better with a gun than she was, but if he got close and aimed for center mass she'd be just as dead as if a sniper had targeted her from afar. Another shot, another spit of sand.

And then as she reached the base of the towering headland, the roar of a lion split the morning, shattering any peace that might once have been found there. She whirled around to face him. A month ago, she would have hidden her face in the side of cliff and waited for death to claim her. Now, having made her bid for freedom and being here in Otter Cove for two days, she would face her end with dignity and courage.

Kurt stopped less than ten feet away from her. He raised the gun and took aim. "Goodbye, bi…"

The last word was cut off by his scream as some kind of enormous prehistoric lion leaped through the air and pounced on Kurt's back—the impact making him lose his hold on the gun which went flying away. The beast was huge, far larger than any of the big cats in existence today. Longer and leaner, yet more powerful looking, it had a smaller head, with pronounced fangs and a hump where the shoulders, neck, and spine met like that of a grizzly.

The deafening roar was drowned out by the explosive thunder and controlled lightning of Kurt shifting from man to bear. The lion was thrown free by Kurt's violent shift, but only took a moment to recover before charging him again to engage in battle.

It took only the space of a heartbeat for her to react, but Sienna dove for the gun, rolled onto her back as soon as she had it in her hands and took aim. Kurt and the lion were wrestling in a ball, each trying to inflict as much damage on the other as they could. It seemed that the huge lion was on her side but as she'd never known a lion or even seen anything that looked like it, she wasn't willing to assume it wasn't fighting over her to have as a tasty snack. Sienna aimed for Kurt and squeezed the trigger, the recoil making her hands fly off as she triggered another round. The lion cried out in pain, and she tried to shoot again.

Somewhere in the distance she could hear men shouting and bears growling as they rushed down the sand. She wasn't the only one to hear as Kurt and the lion disengaged each growling at the other before Kurt raced into the sea, and the lion bounded up the side of the cliff, its sharp claws giving it purchase where there should have been none.

An enormous polar bear skidded to a stop beside her, surrounding her with his massive frame and ensuring that no threat remained. Two of those who were in their polar bear form gave chase to Kurt in the water, but he must have come by boat as she could just see him scrambling into it in his human form, weighing anchor and engaging the motor before the two polar bears could reach him. The other polar bear circled around her and the one wrapped around her. They were joined by the remaining members of the team.

"What the hell was that?" asked Wyatt looking up the side of the cliff where the lion had disappeared from sight.

Sienna was buffeted by the violence and proximity of Zak's shift. She leaned into his strength and muscled arms embraced her.

"What is it with you and being naked around me?" she asked as she burrowed closer.

"You have that effect on me. I catch your scent and immediately all I can think about is how bad and how hard I want to fuck you."

The men who surrounded him chuckled, as did Sienna. She knew that was a completely inappropriate thing for him to say, but right now, safely tucked into his body, she didn't much care.

"Annie?" she asked, realizing all of his men were with them.

"We thought she was with you. Derek, find Annie."

"On it," Derek said before sprinting away.

"Wyatt, you take the other three bears. The rest of you, come with me. Let's get what we need from Annie's store and then take Cicely back to the light-house and get to work. Lock up and put up a sign that the store is closed for the day. Get our people working on upgrading the alarm system. I need to speak with Sienna in private, and then we'll join you."

"What about the bears in the jail? I mean we gave them some protein bars and water…"

"Then they'll be fine for now. I'll give Des a call and let him babysit them today. I want him long gone before nightfall."

Grabbing his jeans from one of his men, he pulled them on, scooped her up out of the sand and then walked back toward the store and the relative safety of Otter Cove during daylight hours. Walked was something of a misnomer; what Zak really did was stalk. She could feel the anger in every footstep and had a sneaky suspicion she knew just what this private talk might include. Instead of recoiling from the thought of her mate disciplining her—when the hell had she accepted that he was her mate, and she wasn't going anywhere?—the idea produced a response of arousal. She'd hoped maybe he would fail to notice that; she was wrong, as evidenced by the answering lust that roared down the bonding link.

That was a weird feeling. She'd never felt any kind of connection with Kurt. None.

They entered the store, and he gave Cicely and the men left with her when the rest had come charging to her rescue an update on what had happened and left instructions as what he intended for the rest of them. He took the stairs two at a time and didn't break stride as they entered the loft. Sienna thought he muttered something about doors, but she couldn't really tell. He strode to the bedroom, closing the double doors behind them before he entered the walk-in closet.

Sienna had discovered the meaning of the term closet envy when she'd first entered Annie's closet. Yes, there were beautiful things hanging on the bars, hidden away in drawers and the like, but the antique fainting couch was what had really caught her eye. It had been lovingly restored and was not only beautiful; it was so comfortable. She had considered sleeping on it and if Zak was going to stay, maybe she should offer him the couch and she could sleep in here.

'Fat chance,' snorted the little voice inside her head. 'This big bad bear with his big hard cock is about to rain his displeasure all over your ass and then, if you're lucky, he's going to make you scream his name so loud, they'll hear you in Anchorage.'

Her little voice could be so annoying… especially when it was right. Zak sat down on the lounge, looking far too big for it. She wasn't expecting him to grab her leggings and jerk them down past her knees or fisting a handful of her hair and dragging her over his denim-clad thighs. She was, for the first time in her life, face down over a man's naked thigh, his cock thumping beneath her.

Without a word, the first hard swat fell, and she cried out as the sound of it reached her ears before the searing pain reached her brain. Silently, Zak landed slap after slap to her naked and exposed backside.

"What part of you go nowhere without my permission did you fail to understand?" he growled.

"I thought it would be safe," she said, trying to wriggle away.

"You thought wrong. Who was the black bear?"

Sienna had never been spanked—not once in her entire life. She'd read about it in some of the erotic romance books she'd tried during the first year of her bonding to Kurt, but knowing he would never care enough to physically chastise her had been the final straw and she'd never read anything romantic or erotic again.

As Zak smacked her ass over and over, Sienna bit the inside of her lower lip to try and keep from crying out and answering his question.

"Who, Sienna? I can't protect you as effectively if I don't know who you're running from."

His large, calloused hand spanked her repeatedly, stopping every so often for him to ask his question again. She remained stoically silent at first and then as the heat and pain increased exponentially, Sienna wailed and kicked her legs, prompting Zak to close his other thigh against her as he wrapped his strong arm around her waist, pinning her in place and ensuring she would feel every strike against her backside.

"Please, Zak, don't." Her plea for mercy fell on deaf ears.

"Who, Sienna?"

"My mate from Colorado." It came out in a rush; shame and humiliation flooded her being—not from the spanking but from not having told him from the beginning, from ever allowing them to force her into a pair bond in Colorado.

"Your mate? You have no mark. I've seen both your hands."

"I told them they might force me into the bonding and into his bed, but I would not speak vows or have him mark me as his. I told him if he bit me, I'd find a way to kill him."

"Good girl," he said soothingly, with a hint of pride in his voice. Zak helped her to stand, holding her between his thighs. "No more secrets or lies between us." She nodded. "Strip."

"What?"

"You heard me. Strip."

There was no way she was going to strip for him after he'd spanked her.

'Wanna bet?' asked the voice.

"Let me explain how this is going to be. You're going to kick off your shoes and strip naked for me. Then you're going to kneel on the seat and lay over the arm and spread your legs. Then I'm going to do what I've wanted to do to you since the first time I laid eyes on you. I can't wait to be balls deep in you."

"I…" she started but was cut off as his hand smacked her backside, reigniting the sting.

"You will do as you're told, or I'll do it for you."

One look at the feral look on his face, and Sienna knew it was no idle bluff. Making her decision she used her hand on his brawny shoulder to steady herself as she leaned down to remove her shoes and then her leggings and panties. Zak leaned into the place between her thighs and inhaled deeply, groaning in delight at her scent. Straightening up, he held her by the waist and watched as she pulled the sweater over her head and reached behind her to unfasten her bra, allowing both to puddle on the floor.

Zak stood, shucked off his jeans and she was reminded again of the difference in their sizes. He was tall, well-muscled and gorgeous. She was of average height but carried a few more pounds than she should, but he seemed to like what he saw as he stood and then helped to guide her where he wanted her.

As his eyes traveled over her body, so hers traveled over his. She couldn't take her eyes off him—his muscles seemed to have muscles. Slabs of sculpted perfection covered his body and his thick, long cock stood at attention and pressed against his abdomen before he pulled her close and it seemed to choose to press against the soft swell of her belly.

"There will come a time in the not-too-distant future, my mate, when I will spend days exploring this delectable body of yours, making you come repeatedly before I ever sink my cock in you. I won't formally claim you until I can ensure you can transition from cinnamon to polar bear safely and that I can be there to take care of you."

"And if I don't want to be mated to you?" she asked, curious as to how he would answer.

"I'll take you to bed and fuck you until you give in and agree to bear my mark."

That took her aback; she'd expected him to threaten her with what she wasn't sure, but being fucked into submission wasn't it.

"I'm not sure that's as big a threat as you want it to be."

He chuckled as he ran his hands up her back before bringing them around to palm and cup her breasts before playing with her areola and nipples. He leaned down, nuzzling her sex and inhaling her scent. "God, you smell sweet."

He guided her into position, grasped her hips, and with a single hard thrust impaled her on his rigid staff. It was in that moment she forgot everything but the man who meant to make her truly his.

CHAPTER 15

SIENNA

She'd been right to wonder if she could accommodate him. He filled her completely. There was not so much as a breath of room left inside her. He drew his hips back and slammed forward again, making her moan and wonder if it was from the intensity of the pleasure or the sting along her backside. Zak thrust in and out, holding her in place as he established a rhythm of dominance that reminded her this was an alpha male polar bear. It didn't matter that he was in human form as he pounded into her hard and fast. She realized that this was part of his discipline. He wanted her to feel, wanted her to respond, but he also wanted her to be reminded who was the one doing the fucking and who was the one being fucked.

Her body produced more than enough slick for the raw, primal mating he intended to inflict on her.

She couldn't move. All she could do was moan and accept his dominance as she offered him her submission. Never before had any man taken her like this. Never had any man enraptured her body so that she writhed beneath him. Sex with Zak was powerful, punishing, and inordinately pleasurable.

With Kurt she'd always been able to keep a part of her separate but not with Zak. His possession of her body was all encompassing, and she could feel the heat of it in every single cell in her body. Glancing back over her shoulder, she watched him watch as his thick rod thrust in and out—her pussy spasming along his length as she came, crying out his name and mewling for him.

"That's my good mate," he rumbled, making her body shudder with need and delight.

He amped up the hammering of her pussy. She knew who she was, knew who he was, and even why it was she had thought to deny him. She was enthralled by the man, the bear, and the way he seemed to be able to call forth her primitive response to his ruthless passion. Zak thrust harder and harder, his cock driving further with each stroke, demanding she surrender anything she had thought to withhold from him. As he stroked inside her faster and faster, she felt another orgasm rising up to encompass them both.

"Come for me." He growled the command. She screamed his name as she obeyed.

Zak thrust hard into her a final time, wrapping his

arm around her waist while he fisted her hair and dragged her head back for a bruising kiss. Locking his body inside hers, she could feel him filling her with his hot seed as he rested on her back and allowed the storm to fade away. He kissed her repeatedly before allowing his cock to slide from her body.

"You have no idea how much I wanted to sink my teeth into you in a claiming bite," he whispered as he kissed her shoulder.

Sienna looked at him and smiled. "You have no idea how much I wanted you to."

"I won't let him have you. If he won't relinquish you, I'll challenge him. He won't win."

The idea of Kurt even trying to best Zak in a fight was ludicrous. "He's an idiot, but I don't think he's suicidal."

"Nevertheless, if you want him dead for what he's done to you…"

She laid her finger against his lips. "No. All I want is to be here in Otter Cove with you, where I belong."

Zak grinned and kissed her again. "Where you belong. I need to take care of some things, including finding my little sister. If she calls you, you call me or Derek," he said, taking her cell phone and realizing it was a cheap prepaid one. He handed her his. "I'll use the one I have as sheriff. You keep mine. I want you to keep it with you at all times. It has a GPS chip."

"GPS chip—can you put one in a human?"

Zak nodded. "Sure, my unit was all chipped. You

want to put it somewhere it won't be located..."
Understanding dawned. "That's how you think Kurt
found you?"

"That would be my guess. Is there some kind of
scanner?"

Zak nodded; his mouth grim. "The vet has one.
I'll send for him and tell him to bring his kit. If he
finds it, he can give you a local anesthetic and remove
it, if that's what you want."

"I do."

"Get dressed, but I want you to rest up here. The
store is closed so there's no need to go downstairs."

"People are going to need to be fed, and I don't do
well doing nothing."

He looked as if he was going to say something,
thought better of it and nodded, kissing her. "I like
doing that."

"What?"

"Kissing you."

"Strangely enough, so do I."

"Why strangely?"

"I've never liked kissing. It felt too intimate, and
Kurt didn't like to do anything with his mouth except
bite me."

"I really want to kill this guy."

"And I'm telling you, he isn't worth it. I won't have
his blood on your hands if we can help it."

Zak grinned. "What?"

"I like it when you say we."

Sienna shook her head and rolled her eyes. "Go do what you have to do. I'm going to take a shower and get dressed and then start working on food. When you find Annie…"

He kissed her. "I will. Take it easy. Where would I find your origin pack?"

"Dry Creek, Colorado."

Zak took his cell phone back and dialed a number. "Deke? I'm going to need you to go to Colorado for me. I'll meet you at the sheriff's office in Otter Cove." He ended the call and handed the phone back.

"Who's Deke?"

"The best recon ranger I've ever known. They call him the Finder—if you've lost something and want it back, Deke's the guy to call. He's an odd guy."

"How so?"

"He's kind of like the love child of a Berserker and the Greek goddess Artemis. I want him to get eyes on Kurt and the others in your origin clan. After he gets back from Colorado, I'm sending him after Annie. I need to find her and deal with Henry."

"He won't hurt her, will he?"

"Not if he wants to live another day."

"You're kind of bloodthirsty, aren't you."

"I can be," he said soberly. "I'm an alpha male polar bear…"

Again, she laid her finger against his lips. "Don't. I didn't say there was anything wrong with it. It's part of who you are."

He kissed her finger. "Take it easy. I've got extra clothes at my office. I'll check in with our men, take a shower and get dressed there."

Zak pulled back on his jeans, kissed her again and headed down the stairs.

A while later, Sienna was just finishing up with her shower when she walked into the closet towel drying her hair and was grabbed from behind. "Sienna, it's me," whispered Annie in a harsh voice.

"Annie? What the hell?" she turned to look at her friend and blanched at the gaping wound that was bleeding freely.

"Don't call out. They can't know I'm here. Can you stitch me up?"

"How did this happen?"

"That's a long story. One that's too long to go into at the moment. If you can't help me or don't want to…"

"What are you talking about, of course I want to help you. You're my best friend."

"Good. What happened on the beach after you were attacked? Where did Kurt go?"

"He got away. He had a boat. It was the weirdest thing… wait, how did you know I was attacked? You weren't there…" Sienna's voice trailed off as she looked at the location of the wound. It corresponded perfectly to the location of the shot that had hit the lion. "But you're a bear…"

Annie turned her back on Sienna and raised her

long, dark hair. "Not anymore." She turned around, tears in her eyes. "You can't tell them. No one must know."

"What happened? Who did this to you?"

"It isn't important. What's important is that no one—and I mean no one, especially Derek or Zak—finds out. Promise me, Sienna. I know what I'm asking. You and Zak belong together, but I can't let them know. If they find out, I'll have to leave."

"I know I haven't known either of them for very long…"

"Zak is your fated mate. You two know each other in a way most never will. Are you going to help me?"

Sienna shook her head. "Right. Sit down. Do you have a first aid kit?"

"Yeah, bottom drawer over on the right."

Sienna retrieved the box that contained everything she would need. It had been curated and wasn't something that was pre-made. There was a suturing kit, forceps, injectable and oral antibiotics, painkillers —everything someone would need to avoid seeing a doctor.

"I'm not sure I'm qualified to do this."

"You're fine. The bullet only grazed me and it's starting to heal, but still, I appreciate you looking at it and getting it cleaned up."

"Don't you think they're going to notice you've been injured?" Annie said nothing. "Annie, there's no way your brothers won't notice—maybe not Derek, but Zak will know, for sure."

Again, Annie said nothing before taking a deep breath. "They can't notice if I'm not here."

"Annie, you can't. I don't care what you did, or what you think you did, Zak and Derek love you. They won't turn their backs on you."

"Do my brothers love me? Absolutely. But male shifters get funny about the whole claimed and mated thing. If they see that bite…"

"Is he still around? What the hell kind of lion was that anyway?"

"Cave lion. They are, or I guess we are, prehistoric. The purebloods died out thousands of years ago, but the shifters managed to survive—just barely. There's only a handful left, and the males outnumber the females almost twenty to one."

"So, one of them claimed you?"

"Yes. I got away, but not before he bit me. I wandered for days in glaciers. I fell down a crevasse and thought I was going to die, but I didn't. My lioness saved me and then got us out of there. I'd known about the Shadow Sisters for a long time. My mother was one of them."

"I thought your brother…"

"Killed the poacher who killed her? That's what they led him to believe. The man Zak killed did murder our mother, but he was no poacher. He found out our mother helped his daughter escape the fate he had planned for her. My mother stopped him, and he killed her for it."

"You're going to have them get you out."

"I don't have a choice and I don't have time to give you all the details. Just believe that I know what I'm doing. I left a power of attorney and the deed to this place to Zak. At the time, I didn't know that I could trust Derek. With you here, this place can flourish. It can be all I ever dreamed it would be. Take care of them for me. You can't tell them any of it—the lion, our mother, my connection with the Shadow Sisters. None of it."

"Don't ask me to lie to him."

"I'm not. Just don't volunteer anything and don't answer him if he starts to question you. Tell him that you promised me that. Zak might be pissed, but he'll respect that. He won't like it, but he'll respect it."

Sienna hugged her, careful of the wound. "I just got you back, and now you're leaving."

"I'm sorry about that, but at least I got you and Zak together. You are together, right?"

Sienna nodded. "Yes, your brother is my fated mate, and we will seal that once he's dealt with Kurt."

"And Henry. He won't want you in the middle or Henry breathing down your neck, but he loves you." Annie stood. "Take care of them for me."

She started for the door.

"Wait. You need to pack…"

"No, I don't. I can't take any of this life with me.

Don't look so glum. I'll find somewhere warm to build a new life. I'll be fine." Annie pulled her into a hug and held her for a minute. "Be happy," she whispered.

"I love you," said Sienna.

"I love you, too. Name one of your daughters for me."

"I promise. And I'll continue to channel money and assistance to the Shadow Sisters."

Annie smiled. "I knew I could count on you."

Sienna watched as Annie went back down the side of the house in the same way she'd come up. No one saw her as she crossed the open expanse and then disappeared into the tree line. Sienna wanted desperately to call Zak and tell him his sister was in trouble, but that wasn't her secret to tell. Instead, she would hold the memory of her friend close, name her first-born daughter for her, and make a life with Annie's brother.

CHAPTER 16

SIENNA

*S*ienna spent the rest of the day between alternate bouts of crying and fixing food. Each time someone came up the stairs into the loft, she managed to stem the tears and make herself look passable. She had no doubt Zak would see through it, but she would deal with that when it happened. In the interim, she would give Annie as much time as she could. Finally, at the end of the day, Zak dragged himself upstairs.

"You looked exhausted. Let me get you something to eat," she said as he reached the top of the stairs and wordlessly joined her in the kitchen, enfolding her in his arms and just breathing her in. It would seem her evening was about to go downhill far more quickly than she'd thought it might.

"Where is she?" he asked his hard cock pressing against his fly as it tried to get to her.

"I don't know."

He swatted her backside. "Don't lie to me."

She brought her knee up—after all the thing was a pretty good-sized target. He was able to deflect her maneuver, so she ended up kneeing his thigh. He backed her into the wall, holding her wrists above her head with one hand and her chin with the other. She could feel his cock pressing against her belly.

"Don't try that again," he snarled. "Now, answer me. Where is Annie?"

"I don't like being called a liar. I told you; I don't know."

Sienna struggled and tried to break free to no avail. He was just so much bigger and stronger than she was, and right now he was righteously angry at her. And therein lay the problem. She didn't want to fight him; she wanted to comfort him. He was hurting and there was little she could do for him but to help him work off his rage and anxiety.

She could feel his arousal running down the link that already existed. He was angry and aroused and he needed her. She wasn't angry with him, but she understood what he was feeling and why. Right now, all he could see was that she wasn't helping him find his sister. She couldn't. She truly didn't know where Annie was, but she could offer him something… herself.

Taking his hand, she walked to the large, comfortable couch. She slowly removed her clothes—not in some kind of mock strip tease, but so that she could focus his attention on her. She had found far more intimacy with him in just a few days than she'd ever found before. Once she was naked, Sienna laid back, spreading her thighs so that he could see the glistening honey at the mouth of her core.

The feral grin he gave her was all dominant alpha male. "I think you said something about feeding me."

"Are you hungry?" she teased provocatively.

"Starving. And I haven't ever had such a tempting buffet laid out before me."

"If you're willing to settle for such meager fare…"

"Looking to have me spank you again before I get down to feasting on you?"

"I'd prefer to pass on that portion of the evening's entertainment."

She needed to get him to focus on her and the pleasure he could wring from her body. They could make this work. She could make him understand that Annie was gone but safe and that he needn't worry about her anymore. Sienna knew a part of him would always worry, as would she. He wasn't alone any longer either. Even though so many people looked to him for his leadership, she thought he had probably been even more alone than she. At least no one had wanted anything from her.

"Then you'd best make me understand how hot you know you are—how difficult it is for me to even think about you and not want you under me taking

my cock as hard as I can give it to you. Do you understand me?"

"I hear a lot of talking but am not seeing much
action. I'm starting to believe maybe you don't want
me that much."

The tsunami of lust that came down the link all
but overwhelmed her.

He chuckled—a disarming sound that made her
tremble. "Do you have any idea how gorgeous you
are? How fuckable? Do you understand that I have to
force myself to think of something besides how much
I want to get back inside you? Do you?"

"I'm beginning to, but why don't you come
show me?"

Zak was undressed and stretching out along her
body before she could take so much as another
breath. He pressed his lips against her, his tongue
darting past her teeth in a luxurious kiss that made
every cell in her body come online in a way it never
had before. Their tongues tangled and warmth and
desire flowed throughout her body.

"I missed you today," he murmured against her
lips.

"I missed you more, and I still don't know where
she is."

He chuckled. "That's not why I said that, any
more than why I'm going to tell you I love you. I
believe you. I think you know more than you're saying
but I don't think you're lying to me. I also think you

wouldn't even do that if it wasn't because Annie asked you not to tell—that is not to tell me what you do know. That's okay baby, I'm good at interrogation."

She laughed softly. "Will there be handcuffs involved?"

"You bet. That's why I want you home. I'll handcuff you to our bed and keep you there for days, torturing you in all the ways you're going to love."

His cock was pressing against her pussy. If she could just maneuver a little and get him to thrust up, he'd be up inside her and she could forget all that was wrong right now and just focus on what was right.

Zak nibbled on her lower lip before moving down her body—kissing, nipping, licking, and sucking. His lips found her areola while his tongue swirled around her nipple, before giving it the edge of his teeth. Sienna hissed and forced herself to lie still as he explored her body with his mouth. There would come a day when she would demand equal time, but for now it felt hedonistic to let him have his way and tell herself she was doing it all for him.

As he dropped so that his head hovered over her sex, he gently lifted each leg over his shoulder, nuzzling her labia as he did so before sucking her swollen clit into his mouth. She cried out and arched her body as she came for him. Her body was ripe and soft. She knew he could smell her arousal as he nuzzled her sex. He was driving her wild.

He barely let her come down from that orgasm

before he started kindling another. He lapped up her honey before spearing her pussy with his tongue, tickling it as far as his tongue would allow. Thank god his cock was bigger and longer than his tongue. He reached up to play with her nipples, pinching and tugging on them and humming against her sex—small vibrations that had her shaking and crying out a second time.

Zak rolled up on his knees, gazing down at her flushed body and what she was sure was the evidence of the climax he'd just given her glazing the mouth of her pussy.

"You have no idea how insanely gorgeous you are, but I'm going to make you believe."

He crawled back up her body, settling himself between her thighs and repositioning her legs so they were wrapped around him. Zak rocked back and forth, sliding his cock through her honey, coating it and inflaming her clit. Reaching beneath her, he grasped the globes of her ass as he thrust up and into her in a single pass.

Sienna tightened around him, desperate to have him start stroking her, her nails raking his back. He drew back, kissing her only to break the kiss as he drove back in. Over and over, he pushed into her, only to draw back and penetrate her to her core, his cock sliding over her G-spot again and again.

When she clamped down on him again and she screamed his name, he pounded into her until sweet relief assuaged his system as his orgasm broke over him and he flooded her pussy with his seed, allowing nothing but pure pleasure infuse them both. He collapsed on her, giving her his full weight and pressing her into the couch. She was imprisoned beneath him in a trap of her own making, his weight holding her down when she never wanted to get out from beneath him. This was where she belonged.

Pulling her close, he rolled off her and tucked her in next to him.

"What if people want something to eat?" she asked softly.

"They're bears. They can fend for themselves. There are plenty of garbage cans."

She knew that was preposterous and that eventually he'd let them come upstairs so they could eat… wouldn't he?

Several hours later he relented and allowed the men who were still in town to come upstairs to get something to eat. Sienna didn't bother to get dressed. Instead, she just pulled on his oversized sweater that fell to her knees and dwarfed her size. There was no doubt they'd been heard. A part of her thought she should be appalled, but she wasn't. When they sat down to eat, Zak pulled her onto his lap, seeming to want her close.

Derek had called in, and the two brothers had argued. In the end, Derek returned to Kodiak, agreeing to leave the matter of their little sister in

Zak's hands. After several hours of intense negotiation, Wyatt had extracted an exorbitant amount of money from Henry as a fine, as well as community service for those involved, which would include renovation of the sheriff's office and restoration of Annie's store.

Cicely leaned over to her, "You do realize we could hear most of what was going on up here, don't you?"

"I do, and oddly, I don't care."

Cicely laughed. "Oh, you and I are going to have so much fun."

As they were lining out the plans for the next day, Zak looked over at her. "Annie isn't going to be back, is she?"

"I doubt it. She didn't feel safe here, and before anyone asks, I don't know why. I've only been here a few days, was attacked by my soon-to-be ex, and I've never felt safer."

"In that case, I want her things brought back here so there's a proper bedroom."

"I'm fine on the couch."

"You were amazing on the couch, but from now on, my beloved mate you sleep with me. And by the way, don't think I didn't notice that you did not return my declaration this afternoon."

"Oh, that," she teased. "I love you, too."

"Better. I want to get the cottage fixed up, and we'll need to do something with the store…"

"I thought maybe Cicely and I could run it—expand the business the way Annie wanted. We could ride in and out of town with you."

"That's not a bad idea, Zak. It might make Old Henry think we're going to leave things the way they are."

Zak nodded. "I'd like to develop the lighthouse property so our people can leave Akiak but still have a clan. We can get a lot of the materials from Kodiak and what they can't supply, we can have shipped there and ferry it over."

Wyatt grinned. "That ought to piss off the old bastard when he finds out that we built our own compound right under his nose."

"Well, that is one of the things I like best about the plan."

Opting to leave the store with just the alarm system to protect it, Sienna walked arm-in-arm with Zak out to his SUV, where he helped her into the passenger front seat. They drove toward the lighthouse and as they crested the hill that would drop them down to the sea, the aurora borealis began its orchestrated light show, which seemed to have an unheard harmonic symphony. Sienna wondered if they were the souls of some of the fated mates of the shifters who still lived, laughed, and loved together in the great beyond.

CHAPTER 17

SIENNA

Two weeks later, soft light, the sound of the waves, and the ocean breeze filled the cottage she now called home. Annie had found, bought, and set up an enormous and ornate iron bed for her big brother. Sleeping with Zak—the little sleep he let her get, that is—had been one of the most luxurious things she'd ever done. She didn't care that the cottage still needed a lot of work, didn't care that they were all essentially roughing it. No, all she cared about was that she was with Zak, and so far they and their people were safe.

The crackling of the bonfire that lay between their cottage and the sea was surrounded by people who truly cared about each other. Cicely clung to Wyatt's arm, not because she was afraid or that he demanded it, but because she wanted to be close to him.

Sienna was already getting used to feeling Zak's presence along the link, because she sure as hell was never going to hear him. He wrapped his arms around her, pulling her back into his chest, and let his hungry cock nestle against her backside.

"How long have they been together?"

"Almost ten years. Cicely and Wyatt have been in love for as long as either of them can remember. He joined the Navy to accumulate a nest egg. After eight years, she grew tired of waiting for him, especially as she knew how much money he'd saved. Then my sire decided a great way to strike at me was to strike at one of my men. So, he entered into negotiations to barter her off to some clan of Ussuri brown bears."

"Don't polar bears look down on other bears?"

"All except the Kodiak. So, while Cicely would have been forced into a lesser pairing, according to my father, you are moving up in the world."

Sienna rolled her eyes. "Arrogant bastard. Does it ever occur to you that we she-bears would prefer to make our own matches?"

"It occurs to us, scares us to death, and we make more rules to ensure you can't do that."

"You're impossible," she said, trying not to laugh. "I'm warning you right now. Any she-bear comes to me looking for help, I'll find it for her. I know what that feels like. It makes my skin crawl just to think about it."

"Shh, love. I'm not about to start forcing she-bears into bondings against their choice."

"Not even Annie?"

"Is that why she ran?"

"Not my secret to tell. You didn't answer my question."

"Not even Annie, unless she was just being a pain in the butt, which my sister has a habit of being. I wouldn't force a bonding of any of our she-bears unless I figured out she was the bear in question's fated mate and was being difficult. Have you heard from her?"

She knew that as happy as they were to build a new life for themselves and their followers, it still plagued both him and Derek that their sister had not trusted them enough to tell them her secret and let them deal with it. Her heart ached for them and for Annie, who felt she would lose her freedom if her brothers found out.

"No," she told him truthfully, "but I do know she is safe."

"How can you know that and not know where she is?"

"Because the same people who helped me, helped her."

"The Shadow Sisters," he said their name as if it were a curse.

She turned in his arms to stare up at him. "Do not

speak against them in my presence, Zak. I'd be dead if it weren't for them. I have no doubt about it. And if she-bears and others didn't feel they had other options, they wouldn't exist."

"How's the work on the bistro coming?" he asked. She knew he was trying to steer them to neutral ground.

"It's coming along great. It might come along faster if you'd let me go to Seattle."

"Not happening. It seems Kurt lost a lot of face not bringing you home and has no interest in setting you free. I'm going to try upping the ante one more time. If that doesn't work, I'll challenge him. After all, he never claimed you properly, and that's my bite mark along your shoulder."

"Yes, it is. That hurt, by the way. Derek thought you were nuts to formally claim me with everything that's going on."

"That's because Derek doesn't have his fated mate."

"Derek agrees with Wyatt that your sire is up to something, and that is never good for anyone. Did you expect this many people to take you up on your invitation to join us?"

"Derek and Wyatt aren't the only ones who think that. As for the number of people, yes and no. I didn't really expect it, but I'm also not surprised. I appreciate your understanding about putting the restaurant on hold."

"No, we needed to make the improvements here. For what it's worth, the single she-bears love the semi-private rooms, especially since the boys just get a bunkhouse. You're not nearly the neanderthal barbarian you like people to think you are."

"I don't know that I'm not. I've been plundering and pillaging your body to my heart's content for the last few weeks and intend to continue to do it until I draw my last breath."

"You're such a drama queen," she teased.

Zak was all male alpha bear, but he was an enlightened one, and she found she was flourishing under his tough but loving dominance. As she looked up at him, he wound his hand in her hair and tugged her head back, his mouth descending on hers in a dominant kiss. His arms tightened around her, holding her close.

Sienna, in return, clung to him, letting her mouth soften and open under his, their tongues dancing together as though they'd been lovers forever. He pressed his lips to hers, letting the heat and arousal he was feeling permeate her being. She adored him; couldn't imagine how she had lived before him.

A dark cloud must have passed through her eyes.

"What?" he asked.

"Nothin…" The word was never finished as it was cut off by a sharp smack to her ass.

"Let's try again, remembering that your alpha and

fated mate has issues with your behavior when he knows you are outright lying to him. What?"

"Sometimes I worry that I've caused so much upheaval…"

"You have done nothing of the sort," he assured her. "This fight with Henry was always going to happen, and your ex was always going to get his ass kicked."

"You really hope you can't come to an agreement, which I have to tell you—you do realize it bugs the shit out of me that I'm being bartered like an old shoe, don't you?"

"Baby, there is nothing about you that resembles an old shoe. And yes, I'd like to beat the shit out of him. If he pushes it to a fight to the death, I'm happy to accommodate him."

Zak believed there was a darkness to his soul that allowed him to kill. Sienna believed just the opposite —that it was his honor, courage, and fidelity to those he cared about that allowed him to end another's life —never without reason and never without trying to find another way.

"How does Jax think Derek is doing?"

"Derek needs more seasoning. He's still too quick to escalate a situation when there's a better way to handle it. Better isn't always easier or faster. Derek's saving grace, according to Jax, is that he only wants to rush in like an avenging angel when he believes there's a vulnerable person involved—a woman, a child, the elderly, the disabled. So, the instincts are right, just the solutions sometimes leave a bit to be desired. Jax says, though, that all the females in town adore him, even Jax's mate and she's the one Derek tried to poach."

Sienna laughed. "Derek says as much as he adores Autumn, she is far too feisty for his taste. He keeps saying he wants a nice, quiet she-bear like me."

Zak laughed. "Shows how much he knows. You and Cicely have got to stop inciting the other females…"

"We don't incite anyone; we merely point out that they have other options."

"Neither of you are earning any points with some of our warriors."

"Then your warriors need to learn better manners. Derek says Autumn thinks we ought to do mixers so the clans can get to know one another better."

Zak laughed. "Yeah, Jax doesn't want you and Cicely anywhere near the she-bears of his clan, and I don't blame him. The two of you are all kinds of trouble. It's the only time I'm ever glad Annie isn't here."

She laid her head on his chest. "You don't mean that. I know you miss her. I also know you should never doubt that she loves you and Derek, and she always will."

"Then why?" he asked, the pain evident in his voice.

"Because she felt she had no other way."

"Did she doubt us? Did she think we would side with Henry and force her back to Akiak? Do you think if we'd shared with her our plans? Wyatt asks himself that all the time."

"He shouldn't. It really had very little to do with any of you. She believed she had to leave. I wish I could ease your pain."

"You do," he whispered. "You do. Every time I wake to see your eyes, I love you just a little more, and the pain in my heart lessens just a little bit."

Zak leaned down in front of her, pushing the sweater of his that she wore out of his way. The cool morning air had the desired effect on her nipples, and they pebbled prettily for him. He trailed long, slow, hot, wet kisses down her throat, along her collar bones, and down to her nipples. Her head lolled back as she gave over to the sensual intimacy that she felt with him.

He swirled his tongue around her areola, spiraling in until he could tongue her nipples, moving between them as he rested his hands on the globes of her ass, caressing them. He sucked one nipple into his mouth as his hand stole up between her legs to stroke and play. Zak latched onto the nipple, sucking hard and sending electrical charges through her body, colliding together in her pussy.

Grasping the backs of her thighs, he lifted her off the ground, lining up the thick head of his cock so that it parted her feminine folds and joined them together once more.

There was a knock on the cottage door. Zak swore and set her on the countertop before stalking over to the door and throwing it open. Sienna supposed if they wanted to interrupt Zak's morning pleasure before the two of them got Cicely and the three of them went into town, they would just have to deal with Zak's frustrated anger... and that of his unruly cock.

He closed the door and looked weary.

"The asshole who calls himself the alpha of your origin clan has brought charges against you, me, and my father's clan. He is demanding either your return or the payment of an outrageous sum which just happens to be every last dime I have. The council is giving us no choice but to answer to them in Toronto."

"Why would they want to meet in Canada? Both clans are American."

"But the council covers all of North America. They want you there so that the she-bear in question can be returned to whichever mate her council determines she belongs to."

"I'll show them this claiming bite, and that'll be the end of it."

"No. You're staying home."

"You don't believe they intend to determine anything, do you?

"No. I think the outcome has been determined, and they want us on neutral ground."

"Collusion?" Sienna asked.

Zak shook his head. "No. War."

CHAPTER 18

"*T*alk to him," she pleaded with Wyatt for the umpteenth time.

"He's not going to back down, and he won't let them bankrupt us. He'll challenge your ex..."

"Who is not stupid enough to think he could win in a fight with Zak. I'm telling you, this whole thing is not right."

"And he/we know that. We're not taking the council at their word that everything is on the up and up, but he wants you here, surrounded by our men."

"But the bite mark. Kurt never claimed me, we never even did the hand-fasting thing. Trust me, you cannot miss Zak's mark. One look, and that should be the end of it."

"Quit vexing Wyatt. I expect you to behave yourself while I'm gone," Zak said as he set his duffle down by the door. I shouldn't be but a day or two at the most. Try not to be a total pain in Wyatt's ass," he leaned over and kissed her, "or I'll be a pain in yours when I return."

Sienna rolled her eyes. "Neanderthal."

Bud was picking him up in the float plane and her voice caught in her throat as she heard the plane circle and head for the stretch of water opposite the compound.

"Everything will be all right, Sienna. You are safe with our people. Anything you'd like from Toronto?" he asked solicitously.

"Yes, I've changed my mind. I want Kurt's head on a platter."

Zak chuckled, kissed her, and then picked up his duffle and strode down the dock, boarding Bud's plane and heading out to Anchorage, where he'd pick up a flight for Canada. Sienna waited until everyone had picked up and was working on various construction projects before she grabbed a set of keys to the SUV and fired up the engine.

"And you are going where?" asked Wyatt.

"Into town. We have a store to run, and we have a big delivery today. If the big bad alpha can go traipsing off to Toronto, then I can bloody well go into Otter Cove to run the store. Besides which, there's stuff I need to pick up for out here."

"I want an escort for you."

"For heaven's sake, Wyatt, you're being overly protective."

"Do you give Zak this kind of grief every day?"

"No, because he's going into town anyway. I normally don't see him until he picks us back up. Henry still may have his supporters up at Akiak, but no one in town supports him. I swear, if you don't move, I'm going to run over your foot."

Wyatt stepped back. "I'll get someone to come into town with you. If Henry is going to try anything, it'll be while Zak is gone."

"If you want to send someone, go ahead and send him. I'm going to work."

"Wait for me," cried Cicely as she hopped into the passenger seat.

Sienna threw the SUV in gear and almost drove over Wyatt's foot, hitting the gas too hard and making the tires spray gravel until she reached the main road.

"You're not going to be in too much trouble with Wyatt, are you?"

"Not too much," laughed Cicely, who had quickly become a close friend.

They drove into town and had a small crowd of people waiting for them as they parked around back and opened up the store. They had a steady stream of customers and good to his word, Wyatt sent one of their bears into town to keep a watchful eye over them. Just as Cicely was throwing the lock on the front door, there was a knock and Sienna could hear her politely arguing with a customer who seemed determined to pick up whatever it was he had forgotten.

"Can you go up there and give Cicely a hand at getting rid of this yahoo?"

"Sure thing, Milady."

No sooner had the large warrior gotten to the door, than she heard the distinctive spitting sound of two shots being fired and Cicely's scream, cut off by the assailant as the warrior crumpled to the floor and Kurt stepped in, slamming the door behind him.

"Shut up," he hissed. "This is all your fault," he said gesturing to a terrified Cicely and the wounded man on the floor.

Sienna had spent far too many years being afraid —afraid of Kurt, his father, his friends with their greasy paws—and had determined even before she met Zak that she was done with being afraid. No longer would FEAR mean Forget Everything and Run. From that point on, she had determined its meaning to be Face Everything and Rise.

"You're right Kurt. Why don't you let Cicely here go? She is the mate to Zak's second-in-command…"

Kurt scented the air. "You were with him this morning. You reek of him."

"He's a lusty man and used me to alleviate that lust. He does that quite often. I don't think there's a flat surface in our cottage that he hasn't fucked me on. The man likes to fuck."

"Bit of a surprise for him, you don't."

"You know I think you're right. I'm defective somehow. Turns out, I don't like to fuck. I thought it was bad with you but with Zak's big cock, it's even worse. That thing is a fucking monster, and he expects me to put out three or four times a day. At least with you we'd settled into a less strenuous schedule. And you know as long as you don't make me watch, I don't care about the others."

"You bitch," Kurt said knowingly as he flung Cicely away from him.

"Cicely, get Dr. Miller and tell him Tucker's been hurt."

The only Dr. Miller anywhere around here was Mystic River's Autumn Miller, the mate of the sheriff. Kurt swung the gun back in Cicely's direction.

"Here's the deal, Kurt. You can't shoot both of us. Within a pretty short time, Cicely's mate is going to come looking for us. He is not going to be happy that you shot one of our men and threatening Cicely is really going to piss him off. Now me? He thinks I'm at the heart of all that's gone wrong around here. I'm not sure he'd really miss me. If we leave now, and I'll go quietly; we've got time to make our escape. The fact is, Zak will be the only one to miss me, so by the time he gets back we could be long gone."

"Sienna, don't."

"Come on, Cicely, let's face facts: I'm obnoxious and disliked, and you know it's so."

"Well, that's true. But I feel bad, because here you are trying to save me…"

"You? I'm trying to save Tucker. We've been lovers almost since the first." She turned back to Kurt. "What do you say? We can head for Columbia, and you can fuck me all you like."

He came forward, fisting her hair on the top of her head and licked her face. It was all Sienna could do not to puke. "Tie her up and gag her," he said thrusting Sienna at Cicely.

"Not until you let me call the doctor. I can tell him on the QT, but if Tucker dies, I won't go with you. You'll have to drag me along, and I'll make a lot of fuss."

Kurt nodded. "I have a plane waiting. Once we're onboard, you can call. Now tie her the fuck up."

"Okay, Kurt," Sienna said in the same placating voice she'd been using for years. "Let me get her tied up so she won't be hurt, and we'll head out."

Sienna tied Cicely with a silken cord that would never hold a knot. It would slip regardless of how tight the knot was pulled. She just needed to make it look good. "Kurt, why don't we take the sheriff's vehicle. It's out back. I can lock the front door and make everything look normal. We can take Zak's vehicle and drive out to the plane. Who's going to stop the sheriff's SUV, right?"

Kurt seemed to think for a minute and consider her words carefully. He really was dumber than a rock. Driving the sheriff's vehicle meant that anyone seeing them would expect to see Zak. His brooding good looks made him hard to forget. "Okay, that makes some sense."

Once Cicely was tied up, she and Kurt went out to the SUV. "How come you're being so helpful?"

"Well, for one thing, I've seen what it's like being on my own or the mate to another. I think I had a head full of romantic notions, and now I know better. Besides, who wants to live in some tiny town in the middle of Nowhere, Alaska? And don't forget, when you came before, I was trying to run away."

"Yeah," said Kurt, brightening. "Yea. I guess you figured out you didn't have it so bad with me."

"Yes," she said, nodding her head. "I have it all figured out."

She only hoped she did. They drove to a clearing quite aways from Otter Cove. She hoped Cicely had been able to handle the ropes and get Tucker some help. She knew Zak would come; knew he would find her. He might beat her ass for giving Tucker and Wyatt such a hard time, but she would welcome that if it meant getting back to her life.

It was all well and good to say she would face everything and rise, but right now, all she wanted was to have her mate's arms around her, telling her everything would be okay. At Sienna's urging, they parked the vehicle in the lean-to that she supposed worked as a hangar or a garage. She backed in with the front of the SUV facing directly towards the sole plane at the private airstrip. As she got out, Sienna flipped the emergency transponder, which would send out an SOS as a kind of beacon to bring help, and the button for the camera in the grill that would record everything.

She walked with Kurt towards the plane, trying to stumble and make him think her clumsy. He pulled open the door to the sleek little prop plane. Kurt had taken flying lessons a couple of years ago. He enjoyed terrorizing people who came anyone close to their home.

"You first," he said with a smirky grin.

No doubt in her mind he was going to try and toss her out. Unfortunately for him, the cavalry, in the guise of a polar bear-shifter, former Navy SEAL had arrived. She couldn't see him, and she couldn't hear him, but she could damn well feel him.

Midway down the runway, an enormous polar bear rose up out of the tall grass just off the runway, roared its fury into rapidly cooling air, and then dropped back down to all fours. It galloped out onto the runway and charged—it's mouth open, massive canines flashing and roaring as it began to close the distance.

"What is that?" Kurt said, panic coloring his voice.

"I do believe that is my fated mate come to save

me and kill you. I could be wrong, but I don't think so, and he sounds pretty pissed."

The ground shook with every stride the great white bear took; the ground literally trembled. The closer it got, the more pronounced the shaking of the earth became. Kurt looked at the small pistol. There wasn't enough firepower in the thing to stop the charging behemoth. Tossing it into the field, Kurt valiantly shifted into the much smaller cinnamon bear. He looked for a moment as if he would stand his ground, then thought better of it and began to run.

Kurt was making for the tall grass and trees to try and hide. It was probably the best strategy given the size and skillsets of each, but recognizing that Kurt was trying to escape, the polar bear shifted his trajectory so that he could intercept Kurt. The sound that was created when Zak slammed into Kurt was as if an SUV hit a small compact—both made of bone and muscle.

Zak roared and Kurt squealed like a stuck pig. It wasn't much of a battle as battles went. Kurt was clearly outclassed in both size and strength. Kurt was trying desperately to get away, circling back around towards her. Sienna was pretty sure it was to get to the plane, but Zak's blood-curdling roar indicated he thought she was in danger.

Finally, Zak got his paw on Kurt and brought him down—flesh and fur, blood and bone, tooth and claw —as the battle began in earnest. Zak opened his massive jaws, canines glistening as Kurt stood up on his two hind legs. Presented with such an open target, Zak lashed out with his enormous paw and its lethal claws and swiped it across Kurt's midsection, opening him up wide and spilling his entrails on the ground.

Just to be sure his opponent was dead, Zak clawed Kurt again, this time opening a massive wound high on his shoulder, but there was little blood as Kurt's heart pumped no more.

CHAPTER 19

ZAK

*S*eeing Kurt smiling and touching her had made his blood run cold. He knew how his mate felt about him, and Cicely had filled him in on what had taken place in the store. It didn't surprise him as his mate was a creature of rare beauty, intelligence, and courage. She could have done nothing else.

Kurt was down and dead. He would never bother anyone again. Sienna was running for the SUV, what the hell was she doing? Then it clicked, and had he been in his man form, he would have laughed at her. She'd run to get him a spare sweatsuit. With what was left of his energy, he bade his great beast to retreat so that he would have control.

"Are you all right?" she asked, handing him the clothes and checking him for any slashes or bite marks.

He tried to take it seriously, but it really was one of her more adorable traits. Sienna seemed to feel that if anyone was going to get to bite him it was going to be her. And on several occasions, she had raked his back with her nails hard enough that the lines were still visible the next day. When he didn't let that stop him from removing his shirt, she had been disconcerted by the stares of envy he'd received from his fellow bears. At first, she'd been embarrassed until he explained to her that in their clan, marks like that were badges of honor and any bear who could pleasure his mate to the point that she clawed at his back was to be envied.

"Quit fretting. I'm fine."

"How'd you get here so fast?"

"We got word that the meeting was postponed as Kurt had failed to show up. His father was apparently none too happy with the fine they levied upon him. We turned around and were almost home when Wyatt radioed to let us know what happened and that someone had turned on the tracking beacon. I had Bud drop down behind the trees and came as soon as I could."

"Can you walk? That's a stupid question, let me go get the SUV."

The sound of tires crunching gravel and loud engines made her look up, searching around for Kurt's gun.

Zak laid his hand on her arm. "Easy, mate. Those are our people."

She slumped back down beside him and leaned into him as he brought his arms around her.

He nuzzled her neck. "Is it wrong for me to be this stupidly happy when we have a dead body within a stone's throw of us? The council is going to be in a snit because they don't get to decide anything, Kurt's father is going to go ballistic when he hears his son is dead, and he'll have to pay us reparations, my father is up to something nefarious, and my sister is god knows where."

"No, it's not. Kurt deserved to die, the council is always in a snit, Kurt's father was usually in a rage over something, your father is always plotting something, and Annie is safe. I don't know where, but she's safe. I just want her to find her own happiness."

"Was she unhappy here, do you think? Is that why she left?"

"No, and she trusted me to make sure you and Derek knew it. She loved the two of you so very much. I just think she couldn't forgive herself for something I suspect was never her fault."

Wyatt and several of the others rushed to join them. Instead of greeting Zak as he'd always done as either his superior in the Navy or as his alpha in Otter Cove, he instead hugged Sienna close, provoking a growl from Zak.

"Growl all you like," said Wyatt before turning

back to Sienna. "I owe you a debt I can never repay. Consider me your personal doormat in any acts of disobedience you want to engage in."

"She's all right?"

Wyatt laughed. "All right? She's back at the lighthouse breaking out the booze to celebrate the clan's first lady, her bravery, and her quick thinking. The she-bears are going to have a field day with this."

"What did she do?" asked Zak, not really sure he wanted to know.

"Let us suffice it to say that those she-bears who had been sitting on the fence? They just came over to our side."

"At least you're home," said Sienna as she helped him to his feet and they started toward the vehicle.

"As long as you are within my reach, I am home. All the rest will work itself out."

The wind had kicked up and they could smell the ocean not too far away. For now, he would celebrate with his mate and his clan and look forward to the day when they took their rightful place at Akiak and Annie returned home.

EPILOGUE

*A*nnie
Pike Place Fish Market
Seattle, Washington

It was a silly tradition, she supposed, but at the time she had applied for the job, it had seemed like a natural fit. She had gone to work for the world-famous Pike Place Fish Market as one of the fishmongers who threw fish purchased by customers before wrapping it.

Prior to instituting the fish throwing, the fish market had come close to bankruptcy but with the addition of games, fish throwing, customer performances, and national news coverage, there had been a resurgence in business and now it was one of the cornerstone businesses of the famed marketplace. It was a rather mindless job, but it was fun and paid well.

Besides, her real work was with the Shadow Sisters. Annie was now among the regional leaders for the group. She knew places female shifters could start over throughout Oregon, Washington, Western Canada, and Alaska—some in large cities, some in small towns, and some in wildernesses so remote, no one would ever find them.

She based out of Seattle as there were many modes of travel both national and international, so it was often easy to move someone in and out in the blink of an eye.

The cold, cloudy drizzly days of early spring had given way to the warm, balmy ones of the season. She laughed whenever Seattleites complained about the gray days of winter. They'd have lost their mind in Alaska during the polar nights—a time where for more than two months the darkness rarely lifted.

It had been three months since she'd left home. But tonight was about celebrating and believing that love truly could conquer all—except shifted DNA. She'd heard through the grapevine that Zak and Sienna were going to be handfasted tonight. So tonight, she was in one of the many Irish pubs in the city, standing at the bar with a double shot of whiskey. She smiled, bumped her hip to the music and raised a glass to her brother and his mate who she would most likely never see again.

"At last, my mate, we meet again," he purred into her ear, his arm wrapping around her and holding her close against him so she could feel his cock, pulsing as if to the music.

If she hadn't been half-buzzed, she would have sensed his presence long before he had the chance to wrap his arm around and purr down the link to her. Bears had bonding links and they were said to be potent, but they weren't even close to the prehistoric cave lions. A lot of what had gone before between them was enclosed in a kind of sensual mist that was still pervasive in her mind.

"I am not your mate, Deke," she hissed. "Go away."

He spoke to the bartender, who up until now had seemed like a nice guy and handed him a wad of cash. Okay, so he was a walrus shifter. They were usually pretty affable guys.

"Nice doing business with you, Finder."

"You have my gratitude. If ever you need to call in a favor, use the number I gave you. I'll take care of it, no questions asked."

"Good to know," said the bartender as he backed away.

"That's an easy vow to take, given that he'll probably never want anything more than for you to fix a parking ticket."

"Tsk, tsk, mate. You bears have such a lofty notion

of your position in the food chain and couldn't be more wrong."

Deke beckoned to the bartender, withdrew another roll of cash and asked the walrus-shifter something in Irish. Grinning like the fool he most likely was, he handed Deke a key and pointed to the back corner.

"Come, my mate," he purred, "we have much to talk about and many things for you to redress."

"The only thing I regret is ever having laid eyes on you."

He chuckled. "The only thing you regret is my having caught your scent and taken you to my bed…"

"Where you forced your claiming bite on me."

Nuzzling her, he rumbled seductively. "You yowled for me as I drove my barbs into you and took your neck in a claiming bite. You are mine, Annie, and no one will say otherwise or take you from me again. I will not be as easily manipulated."

She knew this band. Knew when they were going to mix it up and make some noise, knew when the music would be rising in a crescendo. She waited for her opportunity, then drove her elbow into his ribs, head butting him as his muscular torso bent forward.

"Nasty tempered she-cat," he said trying to ascertain the damage she'd done. He'd forgotten what a feisty lioness she could be and would need to be reminded of her place. "That is enough. The breeding season approaches. I have need of you. I have secured the old tap room where they keep the best ales. Once I have slaked my lust…"

"Slaked your lust? Who talks like that? You are fucking delusional."

Deke snorted. "Stop swearing, or your backside will pay the price. I don't like it when you use foul language."

"Do I sound like a she-bear who gives a shit what you like?"

"You are she-bear no longer. You are my mate, and you will behave."

"Never going to happen," she huffed.

"Never say never, Annie. You won't like having to eat those words."

"It'll be you who does the eating," she retorted before she realized what she was saying.

The primitive, feral smile that tugged at the corners of his mouth before spreading across his face should have terrified her, but it didn't. Her pussy pulsed in time to the music.

Would it be so bad to have him again? Would it hurt to find mindless pleasure in his arms? What would it be like to writhe upon his cock as he dragged those barbs all along my inner walls? Annie shook her head. *No. Knock that shit off! The last thing I need is Deke Campbell trying to exercise his rights once more. She'd damn near lost herself the last time.*

"With the copious amounts of honey you give up to me, I think feasting is a better term for it."

She glanced back over her shoulder and blinked at

him, finding it hard to believe he'd actually said those words to her. Without anyone offering to help and thinking of nothing else she might do, she grabbed the large glass of ale belonging to the patron next to her, twisted in his embrace and poured it over his head. It would have been more effective if she'd been able to swivel all the way around or better yet, broken free. No such luck.

"You'll pay for that bit of temper."

Annie was now faced with a conundrum. She'd just poured good ale all over Deke's head. She didn't think that was something he would be inclined to let slide. Before she could apologize, Deke bent at the waist, bumping into her midsection with his shoulder. As he stood, he lifted her up, hauling her up onto his shoulder and to a round of applause, he stalked back to where the bartender had pointed.

He opened the door to the small room lit only by small sconces that resembled candles. He leaned over and let her flop onto the table, momentarily knocking the wind out of her. He jerked off her leggings and panties, finding them stopped by the barrier of her boots. He extended one of his lethal claws and sliced through the middle so the sides were no longer connected. The rest of her clothing was as easily discarded before he flipped her on her belly, pinning her by placing his hand in the small of her back while he unbuttoned his fly with the other. She struggled briefly and received one sharp, staccato slap to her backside.

Without preliminaries or permission, Deke slipped his fingers along the petals of her sex. Annie moaned, not in protest, but in need. His answering chuckle reminded her why she hated him. He dipped them inside, drawing out some of her silken honey to rub into her swollen clit. He repeated the gesture again and again. Everything else receded until only Deke, the sound of his purring and how he made her feel. His display of dominance had soothed the ragged edges of her soul once more.

His fingers grew ever closer to her sex, parting her labia for his broad headed cock to barely breach her opening before grasping her hips and dragging her back, impaling her. Annie cried out as an orgasm hit her with the impact of an avalanche. taking her breath away. Never had she been so consumed by the simple act of possession. Her pussy pulsed all around him as he kept still and allowed her to accommodate his size.

"It's been too long," he groaned before tightening his grip and beginning to thrust.

Deke drew back until he was almost clear of her before driving forward again with a ferocity that mesmerized her completely. This is what had happened last time. She'd become so enthralled that she had willingly surrendered her very essence to him. Tightening his hold, he began to pound into her. His cock grazed her inner walls, forcing them to accept and surrender to his dominant claiming. Over and over, he hammered her pussy as another orgasm crashed around her, devastating her with its strength.

He fucked her with a frenzied need, one that bordered on prehistoric. She tried to rise up, but Deke grasped the nape of her neck and pressed down, pinning her in place. She couldn't escape from his mesmerizing control. Pleasure, need, and peace suffused her system as he gave a final brutal thrust, holding himself deep inside as he spilled into her. Her pussy trembled along his length, milking his cock for every last bit of his essence.

Deke withdrew and she stifled a cry from the feeling of loss. He drew her up from the table, removed his own shirt and got it over her head with her arms through the right holes. He cut the rest of her leggings and panties away and smoothed down the shirt.

Once more he tossed her over his shoulder as if she weighed nothing. Annie was too stunned to do anything when he made his way back through the crowd to catcalls and applause, handing the keys to the locked room back to the bartender. Annie was stunned. He'd fucked her and slung her over his shoulder like some barbarian back from the wars with his prize. He made his way through the crowded restaurant her head hung down; she short blonde hair did nothing to hide her face or her shame, as his cum dripped down the inside of her thighs. He was insane.

'*No,*' *whispered the little voice inside her head. '*He's a cave lion and your fated mate.*'*

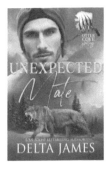

Thank you for reading Suspicious Mate. The next book in this series is Unexpected Mate.

BONUS SCENE

Thank you again for reading Suspicious Mate (Mystic River/Otter Cove Shifters)! This series has been so much fun to write. Zak's character changed as I wrote the story causing a couple of blurb rewrites. I can't wait to share Deke and his beautiful, lush mate, Annie's story in Unexpected Mate. Deke is going to have his hands full.

I have an EXCLUSIVE bonus scene for Zak and Sienna as a thank you! All you have to do is click the link below or scan the QR code with your phone, sign up for my newsletter, and you'll get an email giving you access!

SIGN UP HERE

ALSO BY DELTA JAMES

Paranormal Suspense

Mystic River Shifters (small town shifter)

Defiant Mate

Savage Mate

Reckless Mate

Shameless Mate

Runaway Mate

Otter Cover Shifters (small town shifters/ spinoff Mystic River)

Suspicious Mate

Unexpected Mate

Syndicate Masters

Midwest

Kiss of Luck

Stroke of Fortune

Twist of Fate

Eastern Seaboard

High Stakes

High Roller

High Bet

La Cosa Nostra

Ruthless Honor

Feral Oath

Defiant Vow

Northern Lights

Alliance

Complication

Judgment

Syndicate Masters

The Bargain

The Pact

The Agreement

The Understanding

The Pledge

Box Set

Contemporary Suspense

Relentless Pursuit (Duet)

To Love a Thief

My Fair Thief

Club Southside (spinoff Mercenary Masters)

The Scoundrel

The Scavenger

The Sentinel

Mercenary Masters

Devil Dog

Alpha Dog

Bull Dog

Top Dog

Big Dog

Sea Dog

Ice Dog

Wild Hearts

Stealing her Heart

Claiming Her Heart

Taming her Heart

Finding her Heart

Wild Mustang

Hampton

Mac

Croft

Noah

Thom

Reid

Crooked Creek Ranch

Taming His Cowgirl

Tamed on the Ranch

Paranormal Romance

Looking Glass Multiverse

Shifted Reality

Shifted Existence

Shifted Dimension

Box Set

Reign of Fire

Dragon Storm

Dragon Roar

Dragon Fury

Masters of Valor (spin off Masters of the Savoy)

Prophecy

Illusion

Deception

Inheritance

Masters of the Savoy

Advance

Negotiation

Submission

Contract

Bound

Release

Ghost Cat Canyon

Determined

Untamed

Bold

Fearless

Strong

Fated Legacy (spin-off Tangled Vines)

Touch of Fate

Touch of Darkness

Touch of Light

Touch of Fire

Touch of Ice

Touch of Destiny

Tangled Vines (spin-off Wayward Mates)

Corked

Uncorked

Decanted

Breathe

Full Bodied

Late Harvest

Mulled Wine

Wayward Mates

In Vino Veritas

Brought to Heel

Marked and Mated

Mastering His Mate

Taking His Mate

Claimed and Mated

Claimed and Mastered

Hunted and Claimed

Captured and Claimed

Alpha Lords

Warlord

Overlord

Wolflord

Fated

Dragonlord

Co-writes

Masters of the Deep

Silent Predator

Fierce Predator

Savage Predator

Wicked Predator

Deadly Predator

ABOUT THE AUTHOR

Other books by Delta James: <u>https://www.</u> <u>deltajames.com/</u>

As a USA Today bestselling romance author, Delta James aims to captivate readers with stories about complex heroines and the dominant alpha males who adore them. For Delta, romance is more than just a love story; it's a journey with challenges and thrills along the way.

After creating a second chapter for herself that was dramatically different than the first, Delta now resides in Florida where she relaxes on warm summer evenings with her loveable pack of basset hounds as they watch the birds, squirrels and lizards. When not crafting fast-paced tales, she enjoys horseback riding, walks on the beach, and white-water rafting.

Delta loves connecting with her readers and tries to respond personally to as many messages as she can! You can find her on Facebook https://www.facebook. com/DeltaJamesAuthor and in her reader group https://www.facebook.com/groups/ 348982795738444.

ACKNOWLEDGMENTS

Thank you to my Patreon supporters.
I couldn't do this without you!

Carol Chase
Latoya McBride
Julia Rappaport
D F
Ellen
Margaret Bloodworth
Tamara Crooks
Rhonda
Autumn
Suzy Sawkins
Cindy Vernon
Linda Kniffen-Wager
Karen Somerville

Made in United States
Troutdale, OR
08/11/2024

21934435R00137